COW

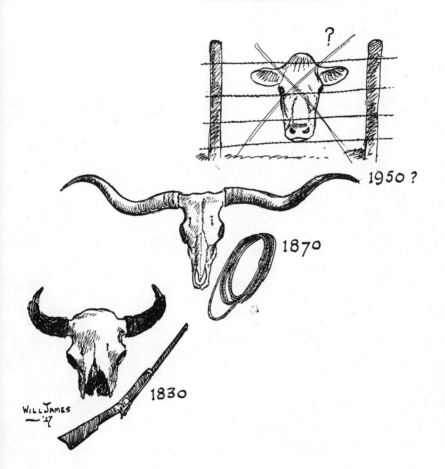

1950 ?

1870

1830

WILL JAMES
— '27

COW COUNTRY

There was times, on account of the snow being too deep, that the cattle
wouldn't always follow them trails. The leaders would
turn back, time after time. Page 240.

COW COUNTRY

BY
WILL JAMES

ILLUSTRATED BY THE AUTHOR

UNIVERSITY OF NEBRASKA PRESS · LINCOLN

Library of Congress Catalog Card Number 27-22183
International Standard Book Number 0-8032-5774-0

First Bison Book printing: February 1973

Most recent printing shown by first digit below:

2   3   4   5   6   7   8   9   10

Bison Book edition published by arrangement with
Charles Scribner's Sons.

PREFACE

WHEN we speak of cow country out here, we mean range country — a country where cattle run loose in open territory and are identified by brands and earmarks, not by names and spots. There may be many horses on the same range, as many as there is cattle, and even some sheep, but it's always called cow country by the cowboys. The words Cow Country mean open range, cow camps, round-up wagons, remudas, riders and branding irons. They mean all that goes to make it a cow country, and when a cowboy says "it's a good cow country," another cowboy gets visions of good range, good camps, good chuck and wages, and good saddle-horses.

According to many plush-seat riders who write, there is no more cow country; but regardless of them, and if a feller wants to, he can start on horseback, not in a car, from away into Mexico and be on open range land from there, acrost the whole of the U. S. — up north into Canada. Of course, there'd be some zigzagging to be done and irrigated settlements to cross, but as I said in one of my stories in this book, there's many places where irrigated or farmed lands are just specks as compared to all the land that's around that's still all cow country. Some of it is still free range and some is owned, but it's hard to tell it apart, because the most of it is open and there's not so many fences to mar the land.

Thinking along on the big scope of earth the cow country still takes in, it all makes writing about it seem sort of insignificant. There's so much to tell it seems, like to cover any part of it right. The people, the stock, the land and the work would take in many big books, to describe half of the goings on in the range country. It reminds me some of an old cowman who'd been in the game for fifty solid years or more, and when somebody remarked how he should know a lot about range and range stock, the old timer said that with fifty more years at the game he might know a little something about it, which meant that for every one thing he learned there was two more come up that was new.

In this book I've took in a few pinnacle tips or high-lights of the range world, it's something of now days, and nothing that I've hunted up. In one story, I tell of a high-class foreigner who bought up a cow outfit and wanted to modernize it to his taste; — that's one way I take of trying to describe cow-country problems. In another story I tell of a show-hand amongst the cowboys. There's also an article on the wild horses and what's to become of 'em. Then there's a story on what happens when a cowboy marries, and a few others. I've tried to describe in my drawings what I couldn't tell in my writings, and I hope I've done a good job.

Sincerely

Will James

CONTENTS

ILLUSTRATIONS

THE WILD HORSE

I

I'D thought it all out long before I pulled my gun out of the holster, and getting down to hard facts, I'd realized it was the best and only right thing to do. I raised my gun slow and easy and, being all was decided on, I tried to keep from thinking on the subject as the gun barrel went up past the target. Pretty soon it would come down again — it'd come down till the sights would be straight in line with the target, and then the trigger would be pressed.

A-shining to the sun was a little white star, the little white star was on a little bay colt's forehead, and that was the target.

A haze of dust was hanging over the big valley, the dust had been stirred by hundreds of hoofs of wild horses, which all was sashayed by many riders. Them riders was wild-horse hunters hired to rid the country of the mustangs, so that cattle or sheep could have the grass the ponies was using. The wild horses wasn't worth anything; cattle and sheep brought good money; so the horses had to go.

As the dust was stirred up in the long runs and left behind to soar above and form a haze, I'd noticed a small object running around through the sage and like it had no perticular place to go. I rode on closer, and there I could make out it was a little mustang colt, just a week or so old. The run had been too long for the little feller and he'd been left behind by his mammy and all.

Them little fellers being left behind that way was one of the main things that kept me from getting any thrill or sport out of mustang running, and thinking on the subject, I've often wished I'd never had anything to do with wild-horse hunting no time.

My horse, seeing the little colt, nickered at him, and the poor little devil near fell down, in his hurry to turn toward the sound; up he came fast as his long shaky legs could carry him, head up, eyes a-shining, and nickering back for all he was worth. The little feller was too young to worry about me; besides, he was so tickled to meet up with one of his kind, that he never noticed me a-setting up there on the horse.

I watched him for a while and felt doggone sorry. I knowed his mammy was running as fast as she could go right then, and away from him; that she was on her way to a trap where she'd be herd-broke with many others and then shipped out of the country. Of course there was a chance that she'd get away, but if she did, she'd be many long miles away before she'd cool down to realize that through the stampede and mixture of dust and many horses she'd lost her colt.

A cow and calf can be separated by many miles, but they always find one another again; it's their natural instinct always to go back where they both seen each other last. But with a mare and colt it's altogether different; they can only find each other for as far as the eye can see, or as far as a nicker can be heard; and when there's forty miles or so separating 'em, as I figgered the case would be with this little colt and his mammy — if she made her get-away — why it'd be plum hopeless that she'd ever

The little feller was so tickled to meet up with one of his kind that he never noticed me a-setting up there on the horse.

find him again. That accounted for, it didn't take no imagination for me to follow on and see what would become of this little feller if I left him to shift for himself. I knowed what would happen. There'd be long days of suffering from the sun, thirst, and starvation, maybe a prowling coyote would drag him down; but any way you take it, the end would be too slow a-coming.

I remembered, and will never forget, when I was in the mustang-running game, how once in a while I'd run acrost some little colt that'd been too young to keep up with the bigger horses and had been left behind that way—specially one little feller. I run acrost him out on a bare white sage flat, and he was the sorriest sight I ever seen a living animal in. I won't go on to describe what he looked like, but it was easy to see what suffering he'd went through.

Being a-way too young to live long without his mammy, he'd had, all of a sudden, to shift for himself in a country which takes a full-grown horse to make out. He'd been too young to look for water, or even know what water was if he found it; bunch grass and shad scale, which was all strange to his stomach, had to take the place, in nourishment, of his mammy's rich milk. A lot of times he'd et plain sage-brush — anything to fill up an empty space. I sort of pictured his lone moping around in the big country; and it's a wonder, I thought, how one of them little fellers can live so long sometimes, and alone that way. This perticular one, I'd figgered, had been away from his mammy for about three weeks, and somehow — I don't know how — he'd made a go of it all that time.

When I rode up to within a couple of feet from him, that little shadow of a colt never raised his head from where it'd been hanging close to the ground. He never knowed I was there; he never even twitched an ear when I touched him, and it was a wonder to me how he could stand up. When I put him out of misery — if he wasn't past that — with a careful shot, I know he never felt a thing, and I only wished, as I rode on, that I had run acrost him sooner.

Now, here was another little feller. I had run acrost him sooner, and before any real suffering had come his way. Now was the time to snuff the life out of him, but I was awful slow; my gun seemed like to want to stick in the holster, and it felt awful heavy as I raised it up careful, to make a sure shot as it come down.

I was finding that it was one thing to put out of misery an animal that's suffering, and altogether another to draw down on one that's young and before the suffering's took holt. Shooting down a little feller so young and full of life struck me as an awful mean thing to do right then; and even though I knowed what was ahead for him if I left him be, I couldn't quite picture it. He was so slick and shiny and so doggoned innocent-looking.

The long blue barrel of my six-shooter was up in the air; then I begin repeating "right thing, the right thing" as I slowly brought it down; the front sight began to get lower and lower. It seemed an awful long while before the points of two little ears showed between that sight, and then I got a glimpse of the little white star, but it was just a glimpse, and no more. For instead of looking where I was supposed to shoot, I was finding myself staring at the little feller's eyes, which was a-looking straight at me and shining. My gun dropped from there, and when it reached the holster not a shot had been fired.

It was near sundown before I got sight of rambling corrals and then, near the foot of a hill, a ranch house. I was mighty glad at the sight, because the little colt, with the little white star on its forehead, a-tagging alongside my horse, was getting awful tired. He'd followed for ten miles or more, and as tired as he was, he showed no sign of wanting to let us out of his sight.

"I sure hope I can find you a home here, little feller," I says as I got down to open the pasture gate. "Yes, I sure hope so, 'cause if I don't, I'd have to attempt to relieve you of living, once more. I know it'd be just another attempt."

An old cowman was just unsaddling as I rode up to the corrals with the colt a-following. He turned as he heard my horse's hoofs, took in all about me, my horse and the colt, and then grinned a "howdy."

"Another little orphant looking for a home, I see," he says. "But get down, stranger," he went on, "and turn your horse loose." It was as I was unsaddling that the old man told me how this was the fifth colt that was brought in by different riders the last month.

"My daughter's been putting in a lot of time trying to help 'em pull through," he says, "but it's no use. These little fellers that's left behind that way are most all too young to live without their mammies' care. Of all of them that girl of mine's had brought in to her, there's only one living, and that one don't look to me like he's going to make it either. There's only one thing to do with them little fellers what gets left behind that way, and that's to shoot 'em soon as they're spotted. But who's cold-blooded enough to do that?"

"Another one?"

It was the girl who'd come up behind us as we was talking; she'd spotted the colt and had come a-running.

The old man turned, looked at me and grinned, "The little feller is off your hands now," he says, "and in as good a care as you could find. Put your saddle away and let's go throw a bait."

"I suppose you're running wild horses," he says, as we start a-partaking of the evening meal.

"No, not me," I says. "I've had my fill of that a long time ago, and if mustang running's got to be done, I'm willing to let the other feller do it. I'll take a cow outfit for mine, even if it is slower."

"I get you," says the old man. "You think too much of a horse to see him crowded into box-cars, shipped to a slaughter-house, and then put on the block to be sold as meat, like any common critter. I admire your sentiments. I feel the same way about it, and so does all of us that knows horses. I can't figger out myself the caliber of a human that'd eat horse meat — to me it'd be like eating my best friend — but that's them kinds of folks' business and not ours — what they eat. The main thing with us is that we've got to rid the range of 'em, so that we'll have the grass for our cattle.

"Right here in these hills alone there's around five thousand head of wild horses. You know how much feed that many ponies use — just as much and more than eight thousand head of cattle would use. It sure is a problem on what to do with them. Everybody is against shooting 'em, many is against shipping 'em out to packing-houses, and you can't sell or give 'em away. What's more, they're accumulating, and accumulating awful fast."

The old man chewed on a while, then stabbed a potato and pointed it at me. "I'm in the stock business," he went on, shaking his fork. "My life's wrapped up in that business. I'm running cattle now, but it's because they bring me and my family a living. Sometimes, I like running cattle, but I'd ten to one run horses, 'cause I like horses best. It don't make me happy that they've turned out as a luxury to raise, and it makes me a doggone sight less happy to see that now they've got to be made away with; but it's come to that, and ——"

Here he looked around to see if his wife or daughter was near. " —— for the good of the horses, the country and all of us in general, whether we be town or range folks, there's only one best way out, and that's for every rider to load up on plenty of ammunition and shoot down the wild horse right where he's born and raised, and burn the carcass.

"That way," he goes on, "there wouldn't be such a thing as little orphant colts like the one you and other riders took pity on and brought in. There's not a ranch, around where these wild horses are being run, that hasn't got a few of these little colts which they try and raise, and for no reason only to keep them from suffering. A few of 'em pull through of course, but it's a long hard pull — and what do we pull 'em through for? We're trying to get rid of 'em.

"But these little colts being orphaned that way is nothing

as compared with other things I hold against mustang running and shipping. Not mentioning the good saddle-horses that's stove up a-running after the wild ones, there's the traps and shipping-pens and box-cars which breaks many a wild one's neck, leg or heart.

"There's only one consolation I get out of the whole thing. Of course it makes me feel pretty bad to see 'em jammed that way after being so free, but the consolation I get, being they have to go, is that the end of it all is not far away for them. I figger that it's a lot better to have them go to slaughter than know of 'em being shipped to horse markets, where they'd be auctioned off, made to spend the rest of their days looking through a collar, at hard labor—and often starved into behaving, and starved some more after that.

"I'll never forget one time I'd shipped a few carloads of unbroke horses to a farming country. I'd went with 'em, had 'em auctioned off and seen every horse took away. I was about a month getting that done, and in that time I seen enough things done to them untamed horses to make me feel like a low-down scrub for shipping and selling them there.

"The farmers of that country was having a hard time. They wasn't at all successful, and their horses showed that; but I've seen many a farmer that was poor and still was working good fat horses. It's all in the pedigree of the man. These farmers I'm speaking of wasn't what you'd call over-ambitious. They shipped their cream, and their children drank skimmed milk, and many other things was done that way, so as to make both ends meet. They lived in shacks that wouldn't make a fair stable, and the stable — why, that was just a few old boards mixed in with strips of gunny sack and held together with barb-wire. That combination made a sort of shelter and pen to keep the stock in; and them's the kind of places my ponies was going to.

"But them kind of places wasn't the worst of it. What struck me most, and right where I live, is the way them farmers would look at a horse. It was in the same way I'd look at an automobile, only with even less feeling. They'd come in the yards with their halters, and after my riders would rope and slip the big halters on the horse's head is when it'd be sort of comical if it hadn't been so sad.

"Eight or ten of them *hombres* would fall on the halter rope soon as my boys was through fastening the halter, then they'd yank the horse out to one of the wagons that'd been brought in, tie him on the back, and with the team, drag and jerk him all the way to the farm. That's the way they broke 'em to lead.

"But the worst was still to come, and all on account that them ponies snorted a little, fought some, and wore a brand. They called 'em broncos and cayuses; and that was as much as to say that they should be treated rough and not given a chance, or else they'd bite or kick or tear you all to pieces.

"Well, sir, I wished them ponies had, before I got through there. I'd see them, once in a while, hooked onto a plow, all skinned and ganted up, and I could tell that while they was being broke nothing much had been fed 'em. I'd heard one farmer tell another that it's the only way to break them wild broncos — not to feed 'em much for a while, then they're not so mean.

"But it seemed like that they treated their old well-broke horses that way too; 'cause all the time I was there I seen very few horses that didn't look like scarecrows. I seen the reason why, long before I left. It was, that to them farmers a horse was only something to plant the crops and harvest 'em with; something to help make a living out of, and with the least expense. To them a horse wasn't considered as having a heart and feelings; he was just a necessary thing to till the soil, like the plow.

"Grain was growed, the hogs was fat and was took to market, but the horse, as long as work could be got out of him, didn't have to be fat. Land was too scarce or valuable to grow hay, so the horse was fed straw, and once in a while a stingy feed of grain. When work was done in the fall, or when a Sunday come that he wasn't needed, he'd be turned out on the county road, to be honked at by passing automobiles and feed on the little grass and weeds that growed on the side of the highways. Right to-day you'll see 'em on the sides of the road that way, and you'll see some with swollen raw sores on their shoulders from the collar, and as big as your hat.

"The bunch of horses I took down that time was the last bunch I shipped. Counting the expenses of rounding 'em up, and then the shipping, I hardly made fair wages; and then, when I left the country where I'd took 'em, the feeling that stayed with me all the way home made the little money I'd gathered on the deal seem like blood-money.

"I swore right there and then that I was through raising horses. I begin raising cattle then, and been raising cattle ever since. The horse is too great an animal for me to raise, and sell.

"That's why I'm saying that I feel a sort of consolation when now I see the wild horse shipped to slaughter and the packing-house. The end soon comes there, and it's a lot better, I think, than having 'em go to the horse market. But what I'm for most, now that the mustang has to go and make room for the wall-eyed cow or the stinking sheep, is this: Give the horse a little consideration, and being he has to go, let him vanish in the country he belongs in. A little bullet back of the ear would eliminate the long runs into the traps, the lockjaw that's caused from them runs, the little colts that's left behind to mope around and die, the broken necks in hitting the traps, the broken legs, and broken hearts, and so on."

Now it's come to the point, in the range States along the Rockies, where the horse has accumulated till he's in the way, and time is up for him to evaporate. But nobody can hold it against the stockman for that, 'cause he's tried to keep the horse as long as he could, and even long after the horse was a losing proposition.

Most every man of the range country that's raising cattle now would be raising horses if they could make a living out of 'em; they like to see them best. They like 'em so well that when the price of 'em dropped they let 'em run and accumulate, and let 'em take up the feed they was needing for their cattle. Then there was hopes that there'd be a market for 'em again sometime. In the meantime the ponies kept on accumulating and begin to grow wild. Now it takes a trap they can't dodge before they can be corraled, and the wild horse has accumulated till in some parts he's threatening to swamp down the cow.

The stockman hates to get rid of a horse like he was a common varmint and a nuisance; but something's got to be done. Times are hard, as it is, in raising cattle, and the effects of the last war ain't nowheres near left the stockman yet.

In one little scope of country here in Montana there's estimated to be around fifteen thousand head of the wild ones. Wyoming has considerable too many, Oregon is overrid with 'em, and about every range country is a-wondering what to do.

An old-time cowman and friend of mine thought of trying to see if he couldn't do something about it, and last winter he went to work building some traps in the heart of the wild-horse country. He caught up his best saddle-horses, fed 'em grain regular and hardened 'em up gradual. After a lot of work and expense in getting men building traps and all, him and his riders finally went to work and started fogging in on the wild ones.

They rode for about two months. In that time they caught around four hundred head, which, after a lot of hard and ticklish riding, they herd-broke and trailed to the shipping point.

There the horse buyer offered three dollars a head for 'em. No bigger offer could be got nowheres. And when my friend the cowman went to do some figgering, he found that every horse he caught had cost him a dollar and a half — that wasn't counting the time he put in either.

I've run wild horses myself one time, for about eighteen months, and the good outfit and system we had is all that kept us from going under. Even at that, we sure didn't come out

These mustangs, if handled right, can be broke and made gentle as any barn-raised horse. They're powerful strong for their size and what there is of 'em is sure enough all horse.

rich, and horses was worth twice as much then. So, as it is now, I'd sure be surprised to have anybody run up to me and show me a bank account, or even a small check, which would be clear money from catching wild horses. So, I figger, if there's any money made on the game it must be the man setting by the desk of some office, and where no sweat or blood ever gets to.

Now that I've got the money part of the scheme cornered, let's give the horse the consideration that's more than due him, and see how all that running, trapping, shipping, and then only to be slaughtered and all, affects him.

There's one thing to be remembered, though, as I go on — it's that these horses are wild. Their freedom means more to them than their necks, and they'll risk anything to keep that freedom. They don't act at all like the good old gentle horse that's hooked to the milk-wagon and which can be led any-wheres without his scuffing hisself. But it must not be forgot either that these wild horses, even though smaller, are a kin and of the same sort as that gentle milk-wagon horse, or what-ever a kind horse can be; for these mustangs, if handled right, can be broke and made gentle as any barn-raised horse. They're powerful strong for their size, and what there is of 'em is sure enough all horse.

Being the mustang is described some now, let's take an average bunch of the wild ones out of an average wild-horse country and follow that wild bunch on through, from the start to where the packing-house marks the end.

Out in a big country of deep ravines, junipers, bunch grass and sage, and at the foot of a butte streaked with layers of rock and dirt of many colors, there's a small bunch of wild horses. Some are dozing and taking in the sun's first warm rays; a few are grazing; and to one side two little colts are stretched out full length, sleeping.

Peace and contentment was right in the middle of the little bunch; they'd been to water at a cool spring during the night and got back on their feeding grounds before the sun come up. Soon now, and after some of the heat of that sun would be took in a little, they'd come out of their dozing spell and start the day of grazing and watching.

The stud — a good-sized roan horse — was already beginning to take in sniffs at the air and showing indications of wanting to move to more open or higher country. He was an old horse and he'd had many narrow escapes from the far-reaching ropes of riders and the traps which them same riders had built to catch him and his kind.

All the way from his thick jaw, along his slick roan hide to his tail, was scars to show that he'd met other enemies besides man. Them scars told some of his meeting up with the cougar, the wolf, and more scars was added on from fights with other studs, either to keep his bunch, or else in trying to appropriate more. Pure black hair had growed on most of them scars, till along the neck he was spotted like a leopard.

The old horse had seen thirty snows or more, but he was rolling fat; and as he started away from the bunch to sort of look around from little higher ground, you couldn't tell but what he was still a young horse. An old mare watched him go and take his stand on the raise, and when the stud, after a spell,

All the way from his thick jaw, along his slick roan hide to his tail, was scars to show that he'd met other enemies besides man. Pure black hair had growed on most of them scars.

turned his head towards her, there was a quiver from his nostrils, and a low nicker was heard; it was the same as to say, "We better go."

At that sign the old mare lowered her head and butted her little colt with her nose. The little feller raised his head and blinked a while, but didn't show no sign of wanting to stand up. It took a couple more jabs and a nip on the withers to convince him that he should, and he looked awful cranky when finally he did get up on them long legs of his. His sleep hadn't been quite over with, and being he was only ten days old, he was needing a lot of that. It was no wonder he was cranky, but as he took on his morning's nourishment of warm milk he begin to lose the mean look that'd been in his eye, and by the time he got through nursing he felt good-natured as ever again, and right up to snuff.

All in all, for a picture of peace and contentment there was none could of been painted that could tally up with the sight of the little bunch of ponies at the foot of the colored butte. Then out of a clear sky, it seemed like, a rider on a tall rawboned horse fell right in amongst the bunch, broke in on the picture, and scattered the peace that was there—the same as if a bomb had been dropped from up above.

There was wild scrambling as the ponies lit into a run. Not a chance did they have to rally any or figger ways to outdo that rider. They just scared and stampeded straight on to where he wanted 'em.

Mile after mile was covered at top speed, coulees, ridges, and sand stretches was gone over and left behind the same as if all was level and good going. Lather begin to gather on the ponies' necks and flanks, and the fear, the fast thumping of the heart and all, seemed to get no relief from the breeze that was stirred. The wide-open nostrils couldn't take in enough air; but there was no slacking down, for close to 'em was the human they feared and hated and wanted to get away from.

The old roan stud kept behind his little bunch and closest to the dangerous human. He was there to see that all kept up on the run, and with the oldest mare as a leader, no better manœuvering could be got. With them wise ones handling things there was a chance that the blind trap, wherever it was, could be located while it could still be dodged, and before it was too late.

It was as the steady fast run was kept up that pretty soon the youngest little colt begin sagging behind. The little feller's mammy, scared as she was, slowed down too, and to keep pace with him. But as the little feller kept a-getting slower and slower, the mother begin to get excited — it was between the fear of the man coming on her and the love for her colt. Then the roan stud, seeing her getting too far behind, took after her to make her keep up. She knowed better than to argue with him, and with another wild glance at the rider and a broken-hearted nicker at her colt, she run on up to the bunch and left him behind.

Twice she tried to circle around and get back to her youngster, which was getting farther and farther behind, and each time she was headed off by the stud; and with the sight of the rider coming on, it was all mighty convincing that there was only one thing to do. Her brain wasn't functioning much any

There was another spurt of speed as the bunch was made to come down over the steep point of the ridge.

more as she was made to join the bunch the second time, and when she glanced back once again and nickered a last call for her little feller, he was only a speck in the big distance.

Many more long miles was covered and then the little bunch, coming to the point of a long ridge, met a sight that chilled the heart in 'em. Of a sudden, riders had seemed to sprout up out of the earth, and from both sides. There was another spurt of speed as the bunch was made to come down over the steep point of the ridge, and then their running had come to an end. There was sounds of woven wires being hit and stretched by the wild ones, the blind trap was tested everywheres, and when the bunch, shaking and wild-eyed, stood to see what held 'em, there was two of 'em laying on the ground, never to run no more. They'd hit the corral too hard and broke their necks.

Shaking and mad with fear, the little bunch fought with one another, and was kept in the trap corral that night. The next day, and along in the afternoon, another wild bunch was run in and corraled with 'em. Another long night was passed, and the day after that, the riders came in the corral, roped each and all of the scared ponies, tied 'em down, and when each of 'em got up, there was one front foot tied to the tail with a piece of rope, and in a way that'd keep that foot useless in running.

Most of them ponies skinned themselves up pretty bad as they fought the rope that held the front foot back, but that was the only way they could be took out of the trap and held together till a pasture fifteen miles away was reached. By the time the wild ponies got there they was herd-broke — that is, they could be turned any way the rider wanted 'em to turn, and the woven-wire corral at the trap done the trick of fence-breaking 'em; for after connecting with that woven wire a few times and skinning their heads up, they'd developed a lot of respect for any fence line.

The riders had noticed, as they came in the trap corral that morning, how three of the wild ones had a bad case of lockjaw. That was caused by the hard run, the sweating up, and then being held in the corral two nights without water. All that comes in with regular mustang running; it's something that every rider hates to see, but it can't be helped, for it's all in the game.

The mother of the little colt that'd been left behind was one of the victims of the lockjaw, and as the riders hazed her on inside the pasture with the other horses and caught her again and took the foot-rope off, there was little hopes that she'd ever come out of it. The muscles along her jaw had drawed up tight till they stood out in ridges, and even a crowbar couldn't of pried her jaws apart.

The riders knowed that water was the only thing that could save her and the other two; and so, soon as the foot-ropes was took off, the ponies was all hazed to a place where the moisture came to the top of the ground and grass was tall and damp. A good-sized creek was close, too, and the ponies that was afflicted with the lockjaw held their noses down to the water and worked their lips so the moisture would make the tightened muscles loosen up.

"They'll be all right in a short while now," says one of the runners.

But when, a few days later, another bunch of wild ones was brought over, the mother of the lost colt was laying dead.

Out a-ways, and by himself, the old roan stud stood, and seeming like never noticing the riders nor the new bunch they'd brought in. The lockjaw hadn't affected him somehow, but something else, and just as sure of an end, was calling him to other ranges. It was his heart which, like his freedom, was petering out on him. He'd hardly moved, and outside of the little water he drank, very little had entered his stomach since that morning when a rider had fogged in on him and his little bunch. A few days later he layed down for the last time.

There'd been fourteen head in the roan stud's bunch when they was first spotted, and now only nine of them was left. There was still the same number, when a few weeks later all the wild ponies that'd been caught, and lived, was rounded up and a start was made to take them to the shipping point. By that time of steady running the riders had caught more than two hundred head of the wild ones, and they was glad to call it enough. Their ponies was getting leg-weary, they was tired themselves, and they figgered that by the time they reached the railroad with the bunch, they'd be more than ready to leave mustangs alone for a spell.

There was long days of travel from the mustang territory to the shipping corrals, and as the riders brought the horses closer to the railroad they begin to meet automobiles. They was in the dry-farmers' country by then, and where there's a fence of barb-wire on both sides of the road, to protect the crops that never grow. Them wild ponies wasn't used to seeing automobiles, of course, and the result was that before the shipping corrals was reached four of the ponies had to be shot, to keep 'em from suffering from bad wire cuts.

There was a couple days of waiting at the railroad for the stock cars that seemed awful long coming. In that time the ponies was grazed on as good a feed as could be got around — that was very little — and finally one evening the stock cars came, and along with them came a horse-buyer.

There was considerable dickering between the riders and the horse-buyer, and some arguments, and it wasn't till that *hombre* showed them how little he was making in handling them horses that the riders finally accepted the price that was offered 'em. It was less than half of what they'd been told the mustangs would bring, and they was losers.

The ponies had to be jammed around considerable before they could be made to go in the box-cars. Many heads, hips and legs was skinned before each car was loaded and the door closed, but finally, and after a lot of work, it all was done and the engine started on its way.

There was three days and nights of travel on the rails, jerking around at the yards and switches, and in that time them ponies was unloaded once, and only for water. No feed was handed 'em during them three days, on account it was figgered they wouldn't bring enough to make the feeding pay. So, as it was, the ponies was sure a ganted-up, skinned-up, and sorry-looking bunch as the stock train pulled in the stockyards of the packing-house; but that didn't seem to matter, for these was only mustangs and in a day or so they'd all be slaughtered and turned into meat, glue and fertilizer. They'd reached the end.

What a lot of chasing, sweating, bloodshed and suffering, to get to that end, and only for the few measly cents each horse might bring! Why take a horse so far away and have him go through so much, before ridding of him? If the wild horse has to be made away with, I think there ought to be some consideration of how that should be done. He more than deserves that.

I had a feller remark to me one time how and what an awful cruel and unhumane thing it was, for a man to go out on the range and shoot off wild horses. I'd agreed with him then, but now, after the running and shipping of mustangs all comes to me, I thinks different, and I've come to figger that the only humane thing to do, being the wild horse has to go and make room, is to have him go quiet and quick as possible — while he's grazing, and right into the heart of the range he growed up on.

WHEN IN ROME—

II

"THINGS are sure a-popping now, cowboys."

Them words skimmed over the prairie sod to where twenty or more of us riders was "throwing the last bait" of the day; and as one and all looked in the direction the talk was coming from, we glimpsed the smiling features of a long cowboy, the straw boss, a-riding in on us and acting like something had sure enough popped. But the grin he was packing had us all sort of guessing; it hinted most to excitement and nothing at all to feel bad about, but there again a feller could never tell by looking at Bearpaw what really did happen. He was the sort of feller who'd grin at his own shadow while getting away from a mad cow, and grin all the more if he stubbed his toe while on the way to the nearest corral poles.

The grin spread into a laugh as he got off his horse and walked into the circle, where we'd been peacefully crooking elbows and storing away nourishment, but now, and since that *hombre's* appearance, all forks was still and all eyes was in the direction of that laughing gazabo and a-waiting for him to tell.

"You don't seem anyways sad about whatever it is that's a-popping," finally says an old hard-faced Tejano.

"No, I don't," answers that cowboy between chuckles. "I take things good-natured, but *you'll* feel sad, old-timer, when some foreigner drops into camp some of these days and *orders* you to roach the manes of your ponies, and brand calves afoot, and tells you that ropes and stock saddles ain't necessary in handling range stock."

The old Texan just gawked at that, and couldn't talk for quite a spell, but finally, after his thoughts got to settling down to business on what Bearpaw had just said, his opinion of such proceedings came to the top and kicked off the lid.

"Any time I get off my horse and begins to pack myself around on foot after a slick-ear," he howled, "I just don't — not for no man. And as far as anybody coming around and ordering the manes of my ponies to be roached, that wouldn't be orders; it'd be plain suicide for the other feller."

There he stopped for a second and squinted at Bearpaw like as if that cowboy was trying to stir him up for a little fun or something.

"But what in Sam Hill are you driving at, anyway?" he asks.

"I'll be glad to tell you," says Bearpaw, "if you'll give me the chance." Then he went on to spread the news why him and the cow-foreman had been called on to the home ranch the last couple of days.

"You boys wont believe me when I tell you," he begins, "but anyway, here's the straight of it: The Y-Bench" (Y) "layout is sold out and has done changed hands."

Here he held on a spell, to sort of let things soak in, and looked around at us to see how that part of the news was taking effect. It was taking effect, all right, but we hadn't got anywheres near to realizing what that really meant to us, nor how it all come about, when old Bearpaw follows on with an upper-cut that lays us all out.

"Some lord or duke from somewheres in Europe has bought it, and he's brought his stable valets along to show us how to ride. And what's more," he went on, "this here lord, or something, is dead set against these saddles we use, so he's brought along a carload of nice little flat saddles for us, and so light that even a mosquito could stand up under 'em."

Bearpaw would of most likely went on with a lot more descriptions of this lord and other strange things, but he was interrupted by a loud snort from the old Texan, who had managed to come to, right in the middle of the blow.

"All right," he hollered, "I've heard all I want to hear, far as I'm concerned." He got up, throwed his tin cup and plate in the round-up pan with a clatter, and walking away he was heard to say: "I've rode for the Y-Bench for many a year, but I feel it that starting to-morrow I'll be hitting for other countries."

No songs was heard during "cocktail" that evening; no mouth-organ was dug up out of the war-bag; instead we was all busy a-trying to figger out how the Y-Bench changed hands so quick, and without warning, the way it had. Just a few days before, the cow-foreman had remarked that the outfit was figgering on leasing more range and running more stock, and now all of a sudden, and when all seemed to be going well, here comes the news that we had a new owner.

"I bet the reason of the sudden change is due to the big price that was offered," concludes Bearpaw. "I bet the price was so big no sane man would dare refuse it; but what gets me most is how a man such as this lord, what was raised on chopped feed and used to eating out of silver dishes, would want to come out here and get down to tin plates. From all I hear, he's going to run the outfit hisself too."

"Most likely doing it for the sport that's in it," I chips in.

"He'll get plenty of that before he gets through," remarks Bearpaw, "specially if he sticks to them pancake saddles he's brought along."

We done a lot of joking on the subject and kept at it till along about second guard, but the next morning things looked pretty serious. Most of the boys was for quitting without even a look at the new owner and lord, though work was at its heaviest, and riders quitting at that time would sure put things on the kibosh for fair.

The old Texan was the first at the rope corral, and soon as the night-hawk had brought in the *remuda*, he dabbed his line on his private horses, led 'em to his saddle and bed, and kept a-talking to himself as he fastened the rigging, his mumbling keeping up till a shadow on the ground told him somebody was near. A sour look was on his face as he turned to see Bearpaw, who was standing close by and sort of grinning at him a little.

"Now, Straight-up," says Bearpaw ("Straight-up" was the nickname the old feller liked best; he liked to have it remembered that at one time he was the straight-up rider of that country, and on any kind of a horse), "what's the use of you blazing away half-cocked, and quit this outfit cold like this? Why not sort of look forward to a little excitement and fun with this lord on the job? I'm thinking there's going to be lots of that when he comes, and that's what's making me stick around. Besides, you can never tell, and mebbe this lord is a dag-gone good feller."

The old cowboy was plumb against it at first and wouldn't even listen, but as Bearpaw talked on of the possibilities, he got so he'd lend an ear, and soon he was just dubious. Then Bearpaw dug up his hole card and says:

"It sure wont hurt you to stick around just for a few days anyway; and if you do stay, I know I can get the other boys to stay too; besides, I'm thinking you'd miss a lot if you go now."

The Texan thought things over for quite a spell longer and finally he says:

"All right — if you fellers can stick it out, I guess I can too; I'll weather it out with the rest of you."

It was a couple of days later and near sundown when Bearpaw pointed at the sky-line to the east and hollered:

"All you cow-valets look up there on that ridge and see what's a-coming."

We all looked, and right away forgot what Bearpaw had called us as we took in the sight, for showing up plain against the sky-line we could see a loaded wagon coming, and 'longside it a few men on horseback.

"That's him and his outfit," says the old Texan. "It's our lord."

"Gosh-a'mighty," says Bearpaw, "it looks like he even brought a manicure with him, by the size of that escort!"

The outfit came on, and pretty soon two riders started on ahead toward our camp. One of 'em was easy to make out; he was our foreman; the other we figgered to be none less than the new owner.

Red-headed and freckle-faced was His Lordship, and as he come close to be introduced to each of us boys, we noticed that his nose was already beginning to peel. His lower lip had started to crack too, but with all his red hair, freckles, peeled nose and cracked lip, there was something about him that was still un-ruffled and shiny, even if it was a little dusty, and that was his high-class riding-breeches and his flat-heeled riding-boots. The little nickel spurs was still a-hanging onto them boots, too, and set 'em off real stylish.

"Well, boys," we hear our foreman say, "I guess Bearpaw told you how the outfit had changed hands; this gentleman here is the new owner of the Y-Bench. I hope that you'll all be as good men with him as you have been with me, and " — here he winked at us — "if a little storm comes up, don't quit too quick, but weather it out like we've always done and don't leave go of the critter till the critter hollers, 'Enough.'"

The introduction was no more than over when up comes the wagon all loaded down, and by the side of it two men as peeled as His Lordship, wearing the same kind of pants and boots, and setting on the exact same kind of flat saddles. Them we figgered was the two that was to give us some pointers about riding.

"Seems like," Bearpaw says to me, "that all their saddles and boots and pants and all are made alike; I guess they all have the same taste."

A lot of opinions was scattered to the breeze, on guard that night. Every time a rider would pass another while circling the bedded herd, there'd be a short stop, a remark passed, and the next time the riders met again on the opposite side of the herd that remark would be replaced by another.

The next morning came, and not any too early to suit us, because we wanted awful bad to have them stable valets show us how to mount a horse or something. There was quite a few horses we wanted them to use while they was eddicating us that way, and we was real anxious for all the learning they could hand us.

But the dignified silk tents with their air mattresses and folding cots was showing no sign of any life. It was near sun-up too, and Bearpaw, being the straw boss, was near at the point of going to the tent and waking up His Lordship, when the cook stopped him and headed him back.

"You dag-gone fool, don't you know it ain't proper to bust in when nobility's asleep that way, unless you're ordered to?"

Bearpaw was half-peeved when he waved a hand at us boys to saddle up. "Well," he says, "I guess we can get along without him."

Them white silk tents was an awful temptation to all of us as we topped off our ponies and sort of let 'em perambulate around with heads free. A-shining to the sun the way they was, sort of invited initiation, and I think that was the way Bramah Long felt when he sort of hazed his bucking bronc' right about dead centre for His Lordship's air mattress. All would of went well maybe, only the cook interfered again, and waving a long yellow slicker over his head, came to the nobility's rescue.

As it was, not a snore was disturbed as we rode on past for

the day's first ride; even the old Texan's loop was spoiled by Bearpaw as it started to sail for a holt on one of them peaceful tents.

"Mighty dag-gone nice of you and the cook appointing yourselves as guardians," remarks the old cowboy to Bearpaw. "I thought you told me that we might have a little fun, and here you come along and spoil the best loop I ever spread."

The morning circle was made as usual and the same as if no new foreman had took holt. So far, nothing had come from him to disturb us in any way, and it looked like Bearpaw had, just natural-like, fell into being a cow-foreman.

Some folks are just lucky that way, and climb up in the world without half trying.

We made our drive, caught fresh horses, and was working the herd we'd brought in, before we seen anything of His Lordship and the valets. We was all busy cutting out when we notices them a-coming like they was riding on the tail-end of a funeral. They was riding the same horses they'd rode in from the home ranch, and to that the old Texan remarked:

"I guess they never change horses, where they come from."

"I don't think it's that, as much as the fact that they're a little leary of what they might draw out of that corral," says a cowboy near him. "Mebbe them thoroughbreds they're riding looks best to 'em, or safest."

His Lordship and his two men came up to within a hundred yards or so of the herd and from there watched the whole goings-on. They sat their horses stiff as statues and gave the feeling

All would of went well maybe, only the cook, waving a long yellow slicker, interfered again.

that if them horses started right sudden, they'd be left suspended in mid-air and still stiff. Hardly a word or a move of the hand was noticed, and as once in a while one of us would ride by 'em in heading off a bunch-quitting critter, not an eye would seem to notice or recognize any of us.

But them not seeming to see nor recognize us that way wasn't on account of their being stuck-up or such-like; it was that they was so interested in the whole goings-on in general that they were satisfied to just set on their horses and watch. Anyway, that's how we took it, for after the work was through and we all sashayed to the chuck-wagon, His Lordship and valets all seemed mighty sociable, and asked a lot of questions, most of which was sure hard to answer.

It was as we was cutting the meal short as usual and starting to go toward the corral that His Lordship stopped us and asked where we was going.

"On circle," answered Bearpaw.

"What do you mean by circle?"

"Ride."

"Why, you made one ride already," comes back His Lordship. "Besides, if you're going, I would like jolly well to go with you, but I am only half through with my meal."

"Oh, that's all right," says Bearpaw. "You can catch up with us."

We caught our horses and rode on out for the second circle, and it wasn't till we got sight of camp later that afternoon that we seen His Lordship again. Him and his two men showed up as we was working the herd, and the three of 'em watched us cut out, rope and brand, with the same interest that'd been with 'em that forenoon.

"I tried to catch up with you as you told me," says His Lordship, who'd edged up to Bearpaw, "but it seemed like you men disappeared all at once and I couldn't find you anywhere. I'm afraid," he went on after a spell, "that I make a very poor foreman."

"You'll get on to that after a while," says Bearpaw; "it all takes time."

The work that had to be done kind of kept His Lordship from carrying on the conversation as he'd like to, and it wasn't till the evening meal was over, and the night horses caught, that he had a chance to get down to bed-rock with us.

He started with a lot of questions which after they was answered seemed to set His Lordship to doing a lot of figgering. He figgered on for quite a spell, and when he finally spoke again, we already had a hunch of what the subject would be.

"When I bought this ranch," he starts in, "it was with intentions of changing and modernizing the handling of it, to my ideas. Of course, it will take time to do all that, and I might need some advice, but if you men will stay with me while I experiment, I promise that none of you will ever be sorry."

"Sure," interrupts Bearpaw, speaking for us all; "we'll stick — we'll enjoy it."

I don't think His Lordship got the meaning of that last; anyway he didn't seem nowheres disturbed as he went on:

"The first thing I'd like to do," he says, "is to make way with them heavy and awkward-looking saddles you men use in

Even the old Texan's loop was spoiled by Bearpaw as it started to sail for a holt on the peaceful tent.

this country." He was looking straight at the camp-fire as he said that, and it's a good thing he was.

"I think your saddles are altogether unnecessary," — the old Texan snorted, at that, — "too cumbersome, and I don't see why they need to be that. We play strenuous games of polo in *our* saddles, jump high fences and do cross-country runs in steeplechases, and I think that, as a whole, we have a freedom to do things from our saddles that you men can't have in yours.

"I have brought some fine pig-skin saddles with me for the purpose of you men using them, and to-morrow each one of you will be given one to use in the place of what you are now using."

"That's all very plain," says Bearpaw, a-trying hard to keep cool, "and being you're so frank in telling us about our saddles, I can be frank too and tell you, before you start in modernizing things, that them little stickers you brought along would be worse than riding bareback when there's real work and real riding to be done. I see you don't realize what our saddles mean to us; but anyway, I'll tell you what we'll agree to do. You got two men with you what savvies all about setting on them pancake saddles of yours, ain't you?" asks Bearpaw.

"Yes," answers His Lordship.

"Well," goes on the cowboy, "to-morrow, we'll all go to work the same as usual. We'll ride our own cumbersome saddles, and you and your two top-notchers can ride your fly-weights. I take it you all have got riding down to a science and it'll be a fair deal. You and your men do what we do, and if, after the day's work is over, you're still with us, we'll agree to use them little saddles of yours and love 'em to death. Is that O. K.?"

"Oh, yes," answers His Lordship, "that will be top-hole."

"And say," hollers the old Texan, "do we get riding-habits with them saddles of yours? It sure wouldn't look right to be riding on one of them things and have to wear chaps."

The break of the new day, and all the excitement that it promised, seemed awful slow coming. A faint streak had no more than showed in the east when us all was up and around. A while later we heard the *remuda* being brought in and corraled by the night-hawk, and we made our way to where the cook had the coffee boiling.

"Say, cook," says Bramah, "better wake up the nobility; it's high time for cowboys to be at work."

But the cook never let on he heard, and there was only one thing for us to do and that was to stick around and wait. There was many a bright remark brought on as the waiting kept up, and all of us was looking forward to the treat we knowed was coming.

The sun was just a-peeping over the ridge, and we should of been ten miles from camp by that time, but it wasn't till then that we begin to hear murmurs coming from the silk tents, and after what seemed an awful long while His Lordship and top hands finally showed themselves.

We'd long ago had our breakfast, so, to rush things a bit, we started out for the corral and begin catching our horses.

"Now, boys," says Bearpaw, "don't all go to catching your

worst horses for this event; just catch them that's in turn to be rode; we don't want to make it too hard on His Lordship."

"And it happens that to-day is the day for Skyrocket," says Bramah, grinning.

Even though we took our time and done a lot of kidding while catching our horses, we still had to wait quite a spell for the nobility to join us. We wanted to give 'em a fair start, 'cause we felt they'd sure need it.

"I guess they miss their grapefruit in the mornings and it takes 'em a long time to get over it," remarks a cowboy; but at last, here they come, packing their little pancake saddles.

"Now," says Bearpaw, as His Lordship come near, "according to our agreement of last evening, this contest is to be played on the square. I'm giving you all the best of the deal by letting you pick out your own horses — most of 'em are gentle; and if you pick out a bad one I'll give you the privilege of another pick. Go ahead now and do your picking; I'll rope 'em out for you."

Quite a bit of picking was done before three horses was decided on. The horse His Lordship was to ride was a good-sized bay and one of the best cow-horses in that *remuda*. He only had one little trick, and that was when first getting on him of mornings, he was apt to do anything but stand still; but outside of that, which is never noticed, that horse was plumb gentle.

The two valets drawed pretty fair horses as to size, but neither one of 'em knowed very much. They was just good "circle" horses. One of 'em would buck, but that was very seldom, and he couldn't buck hard ——

The horses all caught, we started saddling, and had to wait some more there. It struck us queer how it took so long to put on one of them little bits of saddles.

Bramah got tired of waiting and got aboard his Skyrocket horse just "to top him off," as he put it. There was some more delay about then because His Lordship had got all interested in watching that pony buck and Bramah ride.

Finally, the saddling went on again, and the nobility was making ready to mount. His Lordship grabbed his handful of double reins and stepped back to reach for the stirrup, when his horse whirled and went the other way.

The reins being over his head made a jerk on the bit as he whirled, that caused him to rear up, and the next second His Lordship let go his holt on the reins.

Bearpaw caught the horse and led him back to His Lordship.

"You don't handle your reins right," he says; "besides, you've got enough reins and bits on that bridle for a six-horse team."

His Lordship sort of got red in the face at that, but he had no come-back just then; instead, he put his interest in watching Bearpaw, who was showing him how to gather up them reins so he'd have control of his horse while getting on. The style wasn't according to riding-schools mebbe, but it was sure convincing, to both man and horse.

It took quite a little trying before His Lordshp could get onto the best way of straddling a horse, and he didn't get onto it very well, but with the coaching of Bearpaw, and after catching the horse a couple of times more, His Lordship finally did get in the saddle, and there he was, setting like a knot on a log and a-hanging onto all the reins with a death-grip.

All the while that was goin' on, the two valets, who knowed all about riding, had stood in their tracks and watched Bearpaw eddicate their master; then came their turn to climb on. A beller came from the old Texan as he watched 'em reach for their stirrups.

"Where did you-all learn to ride — in a merry-go-round?" he asks. "Don't you know you're apt to get your Adam's apple kicked off a-trying to get on a horse that-a-way?"

Here the old feller got off his own horse and showed 'em what he meant. "Never get back of your stirrup to get on," he says, "not with these horses. If you want to stay all together, stick close to their shoulder and get your foot in the stirrup from there."

The old Texan's talk didn't stand for no argument; every word he said was well took in, and acted on according, because it was realized that what he said was for their own good. One man forked his horse without any trouble much, and that left only one more to contend with.

That last one, though, managed to let his horse go out from under him twice. "It's no wonder," says Bramah, who like the rest of us was watching, "with them iron stirrups a-flapping. I guess they're hard to find."

Near an hour was spent in getting the nobility mounted and ready to go; then Bearpaw took the lead out for the day's first circle.

"We're considerable late getting started this morning," says that cowboy to the cook as we all rode by the chuck-wagon, "and don't fix anything to eat till you see us a-coming back."

From there we started on a long lope as usual, and as we was going over a pretty level country, all went well. The nobility kept up in fine shape and seemed to enjoy it to the limit. Only once did they slack up some, and that was when a prairie-dog town was crossed. The big holes them dogs made looked like a natural place for a horse to put his foot into and turn a flip-flop. Bearpaw caught 'em up on that slowing down, soon as they got to speaking distance again.

"You'll never turn nor head off a range critter if you keep a-looking at the ground," he says.

The country kept a-getting rougher and rougher as we rode, and pretty soon we begin to get in some bad-land breaks; it would of been a good goat country, only it was a cow country. A ways further, and on reaching a high knoll, we scattered; I drawed one of the valets as a pardner; Bramah drawed the other; and Bearpaw took it onto hisself to initiate His Lordship in chasing the cow.

With this valet for a pardner I was hearing considerable about fox-hunting and cross-country runs, as we rode. There was a lot of words that feller said which had me guessing, and far as that goes, his whole talk had me listening mighty close, so I could get the drift, but pretty soon, as the country kept a-getting rougher, I didn't have to listen any more. Sliding down bad-land points seemed to have took the talk out of him.

We rode on till the outside of our territory was reached, and then circled, bringing with us whatever cattle we found. We

As we rode I was hearing considerable fox-hunting and cross-country runs.

had upward of sixty head with us and headed for camp in good shape when, spotting another bunch, I left the valet to go get them, telling him to keep the main bunch headed straight for a butte I pointed out.

The cattle had a downhill run and was going at a good clip, and I figgered this valet, being used to chasing wild foxes, sure ought to be able to keep up with spooky range cattle, but as I topped the ridge and got the other bunch and headed 'em down a draw to the main bunch, I was surprised, on looking back, to see that that *hombre* had lost considerable ground. He was just a-trotting along, and in rougher places would even bring his horse down to a slow walk.

It was either lose the valet or the cattle, and being I didn't want to lose the cattle, I fogged in on them and kept 'em headed straight for the cutting-grounds. I figgered the valet would catch up with me soon as we hit level country again, anyway. There was no way of his getting lost, 'cause the cattle and me was sure leaving a good trail and plenty of dust for him to follow.

When I hit level country and looked back, I was surprised how that feller was still so far behind; he was only a little speck in the distance. The cattle had slowed down by then, but even at that, I'd reached the cutting-grounds and camp, turned my horse loose, caught me a fresh one and was back to the herd with the other riders before that feller showed up.

"What," I thought, "would of happened if we'd been running mustangs instead of cows?"

"Well, I see you lost yours too," says Bramah, a-riding up and bringing his horse to a stop alongside of mine. "This valet

I had, done pretty well, though," went on Bramah, "and I didn't lose him till his horse started fighting his head on account of all them bits. I guess he was leary that horse might dump him off any minute."

We was a-talking along, when here comes Bearpaw. That cowboy had no cattle with him but instead, and a ways behind, came His Lordship and that other valet which Bramah'd lost.

The noon meal came in the late afternoon that day, and it was over with quick. Fresh horses was caught all around, and leaving a couple of men to hold the morning's drive, the second circle of the day was started off in another direction.

His Lordship and the two valets wasn't in on that second ride; the thirty-mile circle of that morning's seemed enough. They was kinda sore and stiff, and the way they'd rub their shin-bones went to show that the little narrow stirrup-strap on their pancake saddles had developed teeth and dug in from the instep on up. We figgered they'd drawed out of the contest and that they was finding how it was one thing to ride around for sport and when a feller *jolly well* feels like it, and altogether another when that same riding turns out to be *work*.

On account of being delayed that morning, it put us late getting in with our second drive that afternoon, but being we had no nobility to keep track of, we made pretty good time. His Lordship and two men showed up on the cutting-grounds soon as we got there, and, mounted on the same horses they'd rode that morning, watched us cut out and brand. Once in a while one of 'em would try to turn back some critter that'd break out, but most always some cowboy would have to ride up and do

He found hisself near straddling that red steer as he headed for the hard ground.

that little thing for them. They was having a hard time sticking to their saddles as the cow-horse would try to outdodge some kinky critter, and they didn't dare let that horse do his work, from which we figgered that the polo game His Lordship described to us as being so strenuous must be kinda tame after all, compared with the side-winding of a cow-horse working on a herd.

A big red steer broke out once and right in the path of His Lordship. Being he was there, His Lordship tried to turn him, but Mr. Steer was on the warpath and wouldn't turn worth a nickel. The light that was in that critter's eyes hadn't been at all noticed by that person, but the good old cow-horse he was riding noticed it, and that's how come that when that pony dodged out of the way, His Lordship didn't dodge with him. Instead, he found hisself near straddling that red steer, as he headed for hard ground.

"Dag-gone queer," says one of the boys, who alongside of me was watching His Lordship shake the dust off hisself, "how a man that's had so much teaching in horsemanship, as they call it, can fall off a horse the way he's done, without that horse even bucking."

"Maybe it's them saddles," I says.

"That has a little to do with it, but he'd a-fell off one of our saddles just the same."

Two grinning riders closest to the bunch-quitting steer started out a-swinging their ropes, with intentions of turning that steer over a few times and to behaving, but Bearpaw, who'd been cutting out, came out of the herd about then and told 'em to put their ropes up and let the steer go.

The boys didn't know what to make of that till Bearpaw explained so everybody could hear.

"We don't want to forget," he says, "that we can't rope and throw a big steer off of them pancake saddles which His Lordship wants us to use, and being we might have to ride on them things later on, we better begin to realize it now, and gradual, so as the shock wont be so sudden."

So the steer was let go, and every other critter which couldn't be turned without the help of the convincing rope. Then that night, while every rider, His Lordship and all, was gathered around the fire, Bearpaw got up in the middle of the conversation and gave us boys another blow.

"I've cut out two cows and a steer," says that feller, "and they're in the main herd. The cows have their noses full of porcupine quills, and the steer has a horn grow ng in his eye. Tomorrow, Bill," (pointing at me), "you can start out with 'em, take 'em to the home ranch, run 'em through the chute and squeezer, saw the bum horn off that steer and pull the quills out of them cows' noses. You ought to get over there and back in three days. Of course," he adds on, "we could stretch 'em out and do that little job right here, but we'd have to rope 'em, and that's plumb past the usefulness of a pancake saddle. We'd just as well start getting used to that now."

Things went on that way for a few days, and in all that time no hint was passed that the contest had come to an end. It was plain to see who all was the losers, but so far, there was no giving in from the nobility. If anything, His Lordship seemed harder-headed about it than ever, and even though the little flat saddles was getting abused something terrible, and stirrup-straps and cinch-straps kept a-breaking and being patched up with baling-wire, there was no sign that they'd ever be set aside.

Then one day Bearpaw got peeved. The wagon had made camp close to a town which was on the skirts of the Y-Bench range, and Bearpaw had rode in and come out with a brand new saddle which he'd had made to order, before he ever dreamed that pancake saddles would ever come into his life.

Bearpaw rode into camp and straight on to where His Lordship was rubbing some greasy stuff over his burned face and cracked lip.

"See this new saddle?" he begins, and without waiting for an answer went on: "well, I aim to use it; if not on this range, it'll be on some other. I've given you the best of the deal and tried to show you how worthless your pancake saddles are out here, and you don't seem convinced. So, to-morrow, if you want to go on with the contest, you'll have to ride the average of the horses *we* do, not the gentlest, and I'll bet that before you get through you'll notice the difference between riding out here and riding out in the parks where you come from."

His Lordship listened to all Bearpaw had to say, but not a word came out of him as the cowboy rode away. We was a-wondering if by sun-up the next morning we wouldn't be all paid off and hitting for new ranges.

It was near dark, and some time after Bearpaw had left His Lordship, that we noticed him a-talking to his two men, and after a while seen 'em all going to where three horses was picketed. We noticed 'em saddle up and ride away, and at that we wondered some more.

We didn't see 'em come back that night, but we noticed the next morning that they'd got back all right, because in the dim light of daybreak we could make out the shape of their horses picketed in the same place as the night before.

Bearpaw was still het up on wanting to teach the nobility a thing or two and he drank his black coffee like he had a grudge against it, but not a word came out of him as he made biscuits and fried beef disappear, until Bramah, who was the last man up that morning, came close to the fire and started reaching for a cup and coffee.

"Did you fellers see what I just seen?" he asks as he filled his cup.

Receiving nothing but blank looks from all around, Bramah laid down his cup and says:

"Come on, waddies — I'll show you."

He took the lead, and we followed him to where His Lordship's three horses was picketed, and then a grin begin to spread on each face, even on Bearpaw's, for on each one of them horses was a honest-to-God stock saddle, and on His Lordship's horse we all recognized the old saddle Bearpaw had left at the saddleshop in part payment for his new one.

"And look up there," says Bramah, pointing at His Lordship's tent.

We looked, and the grins spread, for floating in the morning breeze from top of each tent was a white flag.

MONTY OF THE "Y" BENCH

III

HIS Lordship didn't seem to me to be at all in good humor. Here he'd come from all the way acrost the ocean, covered two-thirds of the U. S.—to the Rockies, brought two horse-valets and a few thoroughbred ponies with him, all to sort of improve on and eddicate, in ways he'd dreamed of handling, a cow-outfit which he'd bought.

He'd paid a big price for the said spread, and he was lord and master there sure enough; but somehow the big, high ambitions he had of improving things, and all to suit him, had run up against some snags which he hadn't at all figgered on.

Considering in general, it was no wonder to us that he did look peeved. If His Lordship could of been present and listening to the way we would discuss the subject of his trying to change the run of things, it would of maybe helped him a whole lot, but that *hombre* hadn't been in the country long enough yet to learn that his high rank didn't amount to a whoop with us, and as it was, he was keeping dignified by having his own private fire and not mixing with us any more than he had to. We was only his hired help.

His Lordship didn't know what a fix he'd be in if we all quit and left him; and he didn't know that we was only staying because Bearpaw, who'd took it onto hisself to see the thing through, had our promise to stick by him for a spell. The work had went on pretty much the same as usual regardless of His

Lordship's highfaluting ideas, and if anything, the break of having him around turned out to be a lot of fun, *sometimes*.

"He's sure strong on modernizing this layout," says Bearpaw one night, as the first guard was riding on towards the herd, "and I'm still wondering how the *remuda* got by so long without getting clipped and the manes of them ponies all roached. I've heard him remark that it would improve their looks."

"If it ever comes to that," says the old Texan, who'd always horn in at such times, "you'll find me breaking this party right now. I can still get plenty of work on cow-outfits that's run by cowmen."

"But," went on Bearpaw, "I'm going to do my best to see that that don't happen; we sure owe it to them ponies to try and keep their respect for 'em that way, and see that their manes are kept intact. It'd sure be a shame to have this *remuda* look like a bunch of livery-stable plugs."

"Sure would," agrees one of the boys, "but I have hopes of us winning in that argument with His Nibbs. We came out all right in the saddle argument, and we're not riding pancake saddles now, are we?"

"Well," chips in the Texan, "that was a dag-gone fool stunt of his—a-trying to make us use them excuses for saddles anyway, and it's a wonder to me how it was it took so much persuading and hard facts before we could make him understand how useless them playthings of his really was when there's work to be done."

Bearpaw grinned and went on to tell us how His Lordship had afterwards remarked that the stock saddle *might* be a necessary rig for range work, but that it'd never do to play polo with, on account that the rider would be hindered in reaching out to hit the ball and so on.

"Me and His Lordship sure went to the mat about that, and I wanted to bet him that there wasn't a thing done in any saddle that couldn't be done in ours," Bearpaw goes on. "We had a contest on the subject; we broke off two willow sticks both the same length and about the size of a polo stick, and we went from there. Before I got through with him, I showed him that with my stick I could reach from six inches to a foot farther than he could, in all ways around, and while the horse was at top speed; then I pulled off a few more stunts he'd never seen before. When I reached down and touched the ground with both my hands and got back in the saddle without a flaw, he seen where he was stumped, and he had no more to say.

"And now, the other day, he was telling me he liked his stock saddle pretty well and thought he'd soon be getting used to it."

But that was just one point we'd won over His Lordship; he had many more on his chest which was bound to sprout up soon; and every time we'd see him riding towards where we was working a herd, we was ready to expect orders for most anything, from giving every cow and calf in the herd a name, to bobbing our ponies' tails.

There was one happening, though, which sort of made us more ready to accept him as being human, and that was his getting rid of them two valets which he'd brought over with him and who was supposed to give us some pointers that'd make us real riding masters. We figgered he was sort of disappointed with 'em on account they was so much trouble to us in having to catch their horses for 'em every time they'd fall off. Anyway, we didn't have to contend with *them* any more. They'd took their thoroughbreds and hit for the home ranch, and his getting rid of 'em showed us that he was ready to dig into the problems of handling a cow-outfit without worrying about having somebody around to see that his boots was all shined up and his pants kept creased.

But as a man who was going to take holt, and run the outfit all by hisself, he didn't do very well. For one thing, he liked to sleep pretty late and we was already out of camp and hard at work three or four hours before he'd ever get up; and if it rained and the weather was a little raw, he stayed in his tent altogether and read, or something. Still, I guess he thought he vas sure enough handling the outfit and being a cow-man.

So far, Bearpaw was given no authority to act as cow-foreman. His Lordship was supposed to be that, but he never was around, and being we wanted to feel somebody was sort of responsible, we all got together and voted Bearpaw on that position till His Lordship woke up to the duties of a cow-foreman.

But I guess His Lordship was so busy figgering ways and means of improving and modernizing the handling of the outfit he'd wished on himself, that he didn't stop to think that he should know something about it before starting to do any changing or improving. Maybe he figgered he'd already seen enough of it to go by, and adding on all what he'd *read* about the West and cowboys long before he'd left his castles, had most likely give

It took real riding when it came to cutting out or heading off a wild-eyed, line-backed cow as that critter quit the herd.

him the idea that he knowed more about range cattle, horses and the handling of 'em than any of us did. Anyway, we sure felt he was short a powerful lot of information, information of the kind he'd never get till he dug in and worked like we did. After a few years of that, he'd then maybe know a little something about it, and we wouldn't have to act as volunteer guardians, like we was mostly doing.

We was there right at the start of his learning, and somehow we felt like it was kinda up to us to see that he didn't do anything foolish, and which he'd be sorry for, after he really got to knowing something. But this looking out after him that way didn't strike us as a very pleasant job. His Lordship wasn't at all grateful, and if anything, he seemed to hold it against us for spoiling his plans. I guess it was kind of hard on him to see that model scheme which he'd planned so careful come tumbling down.

We was right in the thick of branding one day when His Lordship rode up to look at the works — look is about all he ever would do, because he'd learned that the horsemanship which he'd been so proud of when he first come didn't amount to much. He found out it took real riding when it came to cutting out or heading off a wild-eyed, line-backed cow, as that critter quit the herd, and he soon got so he'd just look on and try his best to keep out of the way of the work that took us in and around the herd.

That special day I want to tell about was an awful hot one — sultry and choking; and smell of hair burning as the branding-iron was stamped on the side of a critter sure didn't help to make things seem fresher. We was doing mighty fast work that day because we had a lot of it to do, and from the time a calf was caught till he was branded and turned loose again only averaged about a minute.

I was coiling up my rope and making another loop to catch another calf when I looks around and sees His Lordship a-setting there on his horse and not far from the branding fire. There was an awful dark look on his face, and all the talent we was exhibiting in nifty throws and fast time didn't seem to be noticed by him none at all.

I caught another calf, brought him close to the fire, a-bellering and bucking, and as one of the wraslers flanked and throwed that calf, I had a chance to glance at His Lordship, with the hopes of finding out what was eating on him. He sure did look mad about something.

He had his eye on Bearpaw, but that cowboy was so busy ear-marking, keeping his knife sharp, and tallying, that he didn't know His Lordship was within a mile of him, and he didn't care. But pretty soon Bearpaw spotted him. His Lordship got off his horse and the two got together, and right about then I allowed my saddle needed cinching up, and the minute my rope was free, I rode out close to 'em, to 'tend to it.

I got there just in time to hear His Lordship say that he'd fired Buttons, the horse-wrangler, but he announced it in such a way that it was hard for Bearpaw to understand.

"You mean to tell me that you fired the horse-wrangler?" asks Bearpaw, squinting at His Lordship.

"Yes," he answers, mighty snappy.

We was doing mighty fast work that day because we had a lot of it to do.

"And why did you do that? Don't you know that we're short-handed and that good men are mighty hard to get?"

His Lordship seemed to figger for a spell, and then he came back at Bearpaw with some hard-hitting remarks, such as how he had a right to fire the wrangler if he wanted to, and so on; and then I got the drift from his talk — that the reason he fired him was because the wrangler wouldn't groom and saddle a horse for His Lordship.

"Well, I'll be damned!"

That was all Bearpaw could say, and he come near choking even on that. He stood in his tracks and eyed His Lordship up and down for a spell and then he started on him.

"What the Sam Hill do you think we are out here, servants?" he says. "You came to the wrong place, feller. Where you ought to be is on a dude ranch, where you can *play* cowboy and where you're took care of so you don't get lost or skinned up. If you want servants and petting, you came to a poor place; we saddle our own horses out here, and them that don't, go afoot."

"I want you to understand," says His Lordship, coming to the boiling-point, "that I'm not a dude."

"No, you ain't; you're dag-goned right you ain't," says Bearpaw, looking him square in the eye. "I've seen mighty few dudes, but the few of 'em I've seen, enjoy things as they find 'em out here. No, you ain't a dude; you're just a thick-headed jackass."

Quite a bunch of the boys was looking on by then, and the ropes was all still when it happened and the first blow was landed.

That first blow came from His Lordship, and it landed pretty well on Bearpaw's chin, but not as well as it might of. The result was that it just stirred up the cowboy and gave him a lead, but His Lordship wasn't at all awkward with them fists of his. We could see he'd had coaching there and considered hisself plenty good enough to have confidence.

There was some mighty scientific punches produced by the nobility, and for a spell them punches was connecting so that we looked for Bearpaw to really get peeved. The landing blows was three to one in favor of His Lordship, and it's a good thing, we thought, that none of them punches seemed to land square and to the point, but Bearpaw was no slouch when it come to handling hisself in the act of self-defense that way. He'd been there before, and that wiry frame of his, which had been mauled around by mean ponies, was more than up to anything. No man's fist compares much with the glancing hoof of a fighting bronc.

So, as it was, His Lordship's indoor science seemed sort of insignificant out there in so much daylight, and only went to aggravate Bearpaw, till finally that cowboy really did get peeved. Then come the end, just like that.

We had no chance to take more than one glance at the noble form of His Lordship a-laying there on the prairie sod, 'cause the herd, without a man to hold it, had picked up and left and was scattering four ways. By the time we'd headed off the cattle, got 'em together and brought 'em back, His Lordship had got up, got on his horse and rode away. The last we seen of him that day was quite a ways off, and he was just topping a

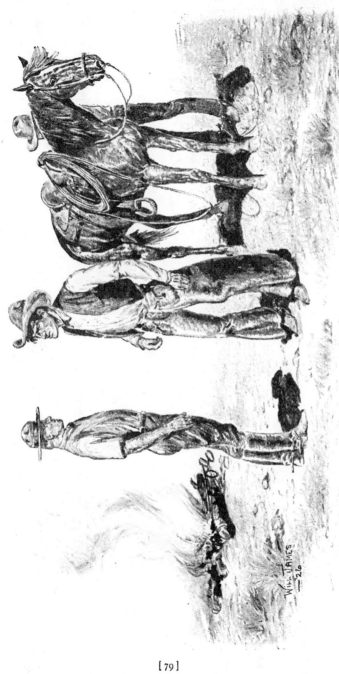

"You mean to tell me that you fired the horse-wrangler?" asked Bearpaw, squinting at His Lordship.

ridge, and he was headed not for camp, but in the direction, of the home ranch.

"Well, boys," says Bearpaw that evening as we was all gathered at the camp, "I guess our jobs have done petered out on this range. Of course none of us are caring much about that, I know, but what I am caring about is what His Nibbs is going to do with all he's got here, the ponies, the cattle, and the country. With strangers handling things, everything'll go plumb to pieces. I know, because I've seen it happen like this before, and it sure is a shame, specially with such a good spread as this one is.

"I guess we been too interested," went on Bearpaw, after a spell. "I should of went at it a little easier, and considered some that lords and nobility ain't used to folks that argues and don't say yes to everything they suggest."

"Yep," agreed the old Texan, grinning a little. "You did hit His Nibbs pretty hard."

Everything seemed mighty quiet at the round-up camp the next morning, but we went to work as usual and with the same interest for the future of the outfit as though we was sure to be with it for the rest of our days. Night come, and no Lordship had showed up. The next day went on just the same, and near a week went by before we seen His Nibbs again.

In that time we'd covered a lot of territory, and we sort of worried how he'd find our camp in case he wanted to, but our worries had been for nothing, because soon as we spotted His Lordship we seen he had been wise enough to get old Jim Larsen to come out with him and find the wagon. Old Jim had been a cow-man since the days when buffalo and cattle run on the same range. He knowed every inch of the Y-Bench range and exactly where the round-up wagon would be at any day of the year.

We was just catching fresh horses for the second circle of the day when the two rode up, and at the sight of His Lordship we all found ourselves mighty busy with latigoes and ropes and riggins, specially Bearpaw, 'cause if there was going to be any howdedo heard, we'd have to hear it first from His Lordship. We was just neutral and sort of waiting for him to show an opening.

"Hello, boys," says old Jim.

We all liked that old-timer a whole lot, and he was greeted according. His Lordship sort of saluted as we turned to greet Jim, but his stiff-handed salute didn't go very well with us; we felt he kind of forced it and that made us all the more neutral. Bearpaw even snorted a little.

Old Jim, his work of piloting the Lordship done, stopped to talk a spell, and then got on his horse and started back. We couldn't get him to stay, and the reason of that we knowed was on account of the heavy feeling that was in the air now that His Lordship was around.

We rode out to finish our day's work, most of us expecting that it'd be our last one on that range. Still, we could hardly expect that, because His Lordship hadn't brought any riders to take our place, and he'd sure need 'em, because the work *had* to go on — there was the main herd which couldn't be let go night or day, not mentioning the *remuda*, which needed a night-hawk and a day wrangler.

Old Jim had been a cow-man since the days buffalo and cattle ran on the same range.

"The new hands might show up to-night," says Bearpaw.

But night come and no strange riders showed up. Us boys gathered around the fire as usual, but not a word was said. Every cowboy was looking at the ground and sort of digging at it with a stick while thoughts of all kinds was stampeding through his brain. It sure wasn't a cheerful evening.

We rode out the next morning without another glimpse of His Lordship; the light in his tent the night before was all that told us he was in camp; and his "hibernating" that way, as Bearpaw put it, was getting on our nerves.

"By golly, I don't have to put up with this," says one of the boys as we loped up on a pinnacle that morning, "and I'm not going to, much longer."

That remark tallied up well with the way we all felt. Bearpaw didn't seem to have anything to say against it, and that was enough proof that we was free from the promise we'd all made that we'd stick with him.

We finished up that day and figgered we'd notify His Lordship that we'd be leaving soon as he got some men to take our place. That evening's meal was mighty quiet, and the excitements of the day's work didn't at all get to be told of and laughed about, nor criticized — as usual — by the old Texan. The empty plates begun to accumulate in the round-up pan; a few cigarettes was rolled; and then Bearpaw stood up.

"You boys wait awhile and till I get the herd bedded down," he says, and rode away with the four riders on "cocktail" to 'tend to that.

There's nothing like the cool air of the evening to help a

feller along to deciding on a hard subject, and we figgered Bear-paw wanted another chance to think things over pretty well before putting a cap on the business that'd stirred him and all of us. It was good and dark when he showed up and then he just went by the camp on a high lope headed straight for His Lordship's light and tent, and tied his horse to a willow bush close by.

All was quiet for a spell as he stepped in the tent; then we hear two low sounds that was like two grunts: another quiet spell, and Bearpaw's voice was heard, low and like far-away thunder.

The steady humming of the voices out there in the tent that night sort of reminded you of an Injun powwow and warriors making medicine before breaking out on the warpath. You could near imagine hearing the beat on the tom-tom, and the whole away off on some creek-bottom. There was a feeling that the old Y-Bench was surrounded and soon now would be invaded and massacreed.

For near an hour us boys was gathered around the fire, and nary a word was said as we gazed at it and sort of pictured there the fall of the outfit that old Pete Garrison had gathered and fought for against the Injuns and sheep-men. Good cowboys had died with their boots on, on that range and for it, and now the whole of it had fell into hands that was going to modernize it and make it look like a dairy farm.

I thought of the colts I'd started breaking that spring. They was turning out fine and I sort of figgered they'd soon be the cream of the *remuda* as cow-horses. I sure hated the thought of seeing a stranger on them. Then there was that good old cow-horse Blaze, which, with a few others, had been pensioned. I suppose with that gazabo's highfalutin ideas of efficiency, and such, he'd be selling them good old ponies for chicken-feed, so as to cut down waste and make things more modern. I wouldn't be surprised to even see him cut down them great old cottonwood trees around the home ranch on account, as I'd heard him say once, that they "made such a mess."

Them gloomy thoughts was a-running into one another that way through this brain of mine, when I heard Bearpaw walking up. I never looked his way, for I knowed His Lordship was coming along too, and I didn't want to look at him none at all.

"Well, boys," says Bearpaw as he come to a stand near the fire, "His Nibbs here, and me, has come to a sort of understanding, and he says he'd appreciate it a whole lot if we'd stay on till spring round-up is over. He's being frank with us and says that he's still strong for changing this outfit to his own idea of what a "ranch," as he calls it, should be like. He remarks that, even though he appreciates advice once in a while, he don't want us to interfere with his plans and the running of his layout.

"I don't know how you boys feel about staying under these conditions," Bearpaw goes on, "but I'd like to stay on if you all will. We've weathered many a storm on this range together, from bullets to sleet, and now let's stick together on this last storm, weather the stock through, and try our best to ship out a good beef-herd, regardless of what happens. I feel like we sort of owe to the old range and the Y-Bench to stay with it till the end comes."

Not a sound was heard after Bearpaw got through talking. I looked up at him as he stood there, sort of waiting, and I noticed many of the boys doing the same. They nodded as Bearpaw glanced around, and then I nodded too.

His Lordship hadn't said a word all the time, but now he sort of cleared his throat and seeing how we'd agreed to stay on, begin to tell some of what his plans was. He'd just started on "for instance," when Bearpaw headed him off.

"If you want to keep these men," says that cowboy, "you better not start talking about improving things, *not just now*."

The next few days that went by was the most natural days we'd had since His Lordship took holt, or I mean since he bought the Y-Bench. That noble *hombre* hadn't at all butted in on our work, and even though we knowed he was going to sometime or other, we felt that we at least had a chance, and that made the trying of saving the old outfit seem all the more important. There was an interest stirred up in all of us we never knowed we had. That interest had no chance to stimulate much while the outfit was running smooth and strong, but now that something threatened to take that old outfit and disfigure it, and no one was there to protect it but us, we sure, all natural-like, stood up for it.

We found we had one strong card, and that was to threaten to quit, but we didn't want to play that card. What we wanted was to get His Lordship to forget them fool notions of his and try to understand — not that we cared a rap for *him;* it was the outfit we was trying to keep a-going.

And now that we seen there was a chance of winning, life on that range perked up and begin to look right cheerful. There was a laugh heard now and again; jokes was told as before; and old Tex's sarcastic remarks was present once more. When the last meal of the day was over and as the big herd was gathered close together and grazed to the bed-grounds for the night, the old songs of the cow-camps and trail-herd were brought to life once more, and as before, the mouth-organ, once in a while, chipped in with a tune.

"Seems like His Lordship is melting some towards us," says a cowboy one day, as the spring round-up was coming to an end. 'Maybe he's getting lonesome sticking around to his tent by hisself, and's got to figgering that, after all, humans can be found inside bat-wing chaps as well as in broadcloth."

It all might of been on account of the spirit that'd come to life at the camp once again, and which made things cheerful and friendly-like, but anyway, we did notice that His Lordship had sure enough melted some towards us.

It started one day with his forgetting his supposed-to-be high rank and setting down on the ground, right with us, and eating his dinner right off the plate on his lap. He helped hisself, too, like any able-bodied man, and when the cook spotted him there amongst us that way, there was an expression in that feller's face that made us look at His Lordship in wondering if he'd noticed it too, for that cookie sure looked surprised, and pleased. There'd been a lot of extra work a-setting up a folding table for His Lordship, and we sure knowed how he hated it. He was a round-up cook and near as helpless at that special job as a hotel cook would of been at the round-up camp.

Now, that was the first time His Lordship mixed in, and he sure had us surprised and wondering, but taking it for granted that he'd at last decided to be sociable and try to be one of us, we sure wasn't going to let anything stand in his way. Old Tex had sort of took the lead to make things seem natural, and in his sarcastic way asked one of the boys "what the samhill" he'd been up to, a-trying to choke the nubbin the way he had that morning when his horse went to bucking.

That brought a quiet argument, 'cause the rider, accused of that disgraceful stunt of grabbing the horn, claimed innocence.

"Go on, you old horse thief," he flings back at Tex, "make up another lie."

The old Texan grunted and went on to *make up* evidence that'd bring the accused rider up as guilty, but knowing that old feller as we did, the whole proceedings only went as a game of matching wits. The two matched so well that pretty soon His Lordship forgot to hide his interest, and before the meal was over he'd chipped in a few comments hisself. They didn't fit very well, but at the same time we thought a lot more of him for them.

From then on, His Lordship was right in the thick of us at every meal. The stone wall that'd been between him and us begin to crumble away, and the time gradually come when his presence there amongst us didn't faze us like it used to. Even the short scrap him and Bearpaw'd had seemed forgotten, and the two was often seen talking together.

But with all the peace that seemed to be with the outfit, we wasn't forgetting that His Lordship still had it in his mind to change things to his plans. He was doing a lot of studying and figgering, and even though he kept quiet and acted more sociable, we knowed that most any time he'd be up with some new idea. And sure enough here he come with one, one day.

It was the last day of the spring round-up. We'd covered the whole range, and the wagon was on the turn, back for the home ranch. We was branding that spring's last calves, and His Lordship had been there to see it done.

"Well, that's the last one," says Bearpaw as he pulled the branding-irons out of the fire.

"And I'm glad of that," chips in His Lordship as he watched the calf get up and lope away towards his mammy.

"I never did like the idea of branding," he goes on. "It seems unnecessary and cruel, and I hope that in the next round-up we have we can think of some other way of marking the animals."

Bearpaw looked under his hat-brim at the few of us that was around and winked the same as to say: "It's come." Then he turned towards His Lordship and asked:

"And how are you going to do that?"

"Well, there ought to be some way," says His Lordship. "I've thought of a few, such as keeping the cattle under fence, or just placing tags in their ears."

"That *sounds* all right," says Bearpaw, "but it don't work so good. Putting a tag in a critter's ear has been tried on the range, and so has other schemes to eliminate branding, and the only result they ever got was a lot of cattle missing and a few losing lawsuits on account somebody appropriated 'em.

"Supposing for instance," went on Bearpaw, getting interested in the subject, "that you was walking on some street with a pocket full of twenty-dollar gold-pieces, and you happened to run acrost another gold-piece a-laying right there on the sidewalk, wouldn't you naturally think it was yours? Well, it works the same way with range stock. When a cow-man rides out on his range and spots a critter with big long ears a-staring at him, and no brand on its hide, he's going to whistle through his teeth at the sight and wonder how in the Sam Hill he ever happened to miss that critter. He'll naturally think it's his—whether it is or not, and he wont lose no time dabbling his line on that parcel of beef and putting his iron on it; then he don't *have* to doubt whether it is his or not. The cow-man that does that is a good business man. He's not cheating anybody, no more than you would be when you pick up that twenty-dollar gold-piece on the sidewalk."

"But," says His Lordship, "what about the tag on the animal's ear? Wouldn't that identify it?"

"Sure it would, if the tag would stay there; but as a rule it don't," says Bearpaw. "Cattle rub 'em off, and there's nothing to show a tag ever was there only a little hole in the ear, or a slit where it'd been caught on a snag and was pulled off. And even if the tag did stay on, look at all the hide that's left without a brand, and it'd sure be pickings for a cattle rustler to come along, take off that little tag, put on a real earmark and then slap his running-iron on that critter's ribs. With all that done, where is your evidence that that critter ever was yours?"

"Bah Jove, that sounds reasonable," says His Lordship.

He thought on the subject a spell and then he played his last card.

"The only safe way, then," he says, "would be to fence the country and keep all the cattle inside."

"You couldn't do that very well unless you want to spend thousands of dollars on fences. Your land is too scattering, and a lot of it ain't worth fencing on account it takes too many acres to carry a critter through, and is fit only as open range. Then again, a fence don't always hold cattle; and if any of your un-branded stuff ever got out and mixed in with the outside cattle, I'm thinking a good many of 'em would be bearing somebody's iron mighty quick and you'd be left without a lot of cattle."

Another one of His Lordship's plans had run up against a snag and evaporated into thin air; he wasn't taking it very good-natured, either, and as he turned to walk away, he was heard to say one little word:

"Hell!"

We was surprised at the sound of such a word from His Highness, and Bearpaw grinned.

"And if it'll help you any," says that cowboy as a wind-up, "I'd like to inform you that the cow-business has been improved all it can, and by experienced men who growed up in the game. If you was to do any changes, you'd find you'd have to cut your herd down to just a few, give them few a name and a barn, and then your layout would turn into ranches, and farms, irrigation ditches, and fences. It wouldn't be a cow-outfit no more."

It struck us as sort of comical the way His Lordship was taking it all, and still it was sad too. We felt sorry for him, in a way, 'cause it don't make a feller feel good to have all his plans scatter four ways, and fall flat, the way His Lordship's had.

"But," says Bearpaw, after His Lordship had gone, "it all stands to reason that a cow-outfit can't be run the way he wants to; it'd be like trying to row a boat on the Red Desert."

That was easy for us to agree to, but not for His Lordship. We could see he tried to take it all good-natured, but it was hard for him to hide his feelings sometimes. He rode by himself most of the way the next day as the round-up wagon and *remuda* headed for the home ranch, and when we got there, he unsaddled his horse and hit for the big house without saying much.

There he sort of hid hisself, and it was a couple of days before we seen enough of him to talk to. That day he stopped to confab a spell with Bearpaw and then got out a big car, telling the cowboy he was going to town.

"Is there anything we need that I can bring out?" he asks as he speeded up the engine.

"Well, you can bring out some salt if you want," says Bearpaw. "It'd save sending a wagon in, and the thoroughbred herd is needing of some mighty bad."

He said he would, and away he went. A few days went by, and when His Lordship came back, most of the boys was scattered out to different cow-camps of the Y-Bench range, riding line and branding up the few calves that'd been missed. A few had quit with the idea of taking on a few contests and rodeos during the summer, and outside of Bearpaw, there was only myself and another rider left at the home ranch. We was breaking horses.

The three of us, and a few ranch-hands, was coming out of the cook-house when we see His Lordship driving up. As he drove his car close to us and stopped, we noticed he looked peeved again.

"These cattle towns don't seem very well aware of the needs of the country around them," he begins. "I've gone to every drug-store in two towns to get the amount of salts necessary for the cattle, bought out all I could find, and had to come back with only fifty pounds of the bally stuff."

"Did you say *salts?*" asks Bearpaw, squinting at him.

"Why, yes," says His Lordship. "Wasn't that what you wanted?"

We hardly believed what we heard, and the only natural thing to do then was to look in the car, and sure enough, the back end of it was loaded with packages and packages of neat little red cardboard boxes, and on each and all of them was writing that told of the purity of the contents and a warning to "Beware of Inferior Brands."

Bearpaw and me both star-gazed at the loadful for a spell, and then we looked at one another. There was a roar from Bearpaw about then that must of echoed for four counties around, and that cowboy just plumb doubled up.

We forgot all about how His Lordship would feel at us laughing that way, and right then we didn't care much. It was too good a joke to take serious, and the only one that was serious was His Lordship hisself. He couldn't understand and glared at us for a minute; then he got red in the face and drove away, madder than ever.

"I'm thinking," says Bearpaw as we walked towards the corrals, still laughing, "that His Nibs don't just appreciate the joke."

Many days went past, and we didn't get to see His Lordship no more. We figgered us a-laughing at him the way we had was a little more than he could stand, and he'd just hit out to sort of live it down, but we was wrong. Old Jim Larsen rode in at the home ranch one evening and stayed the night with us, and he told us how His Lordship had come to his place and visited with him one whole day.

It seemed like, as old Jim said, that His Lordship was out to get information on the general running of a cow-outfit. He had been gathering that from old-timers around, and from all indications was headed out to visit a duke or something who like hisself had left his castle and bought a cow-outfit somewheres in Canada. This duke had been in the country many years; no doubt his experiences would prove valuable to His Lordship.

A whole month went by, then another, and yet no Lordship showed up. The fall work would soon be starting now, and we hoped to see him back soon, but it was away in the middle of September, with the *remuda* gathered, and the round-up wagon, with all hands present, ready to pull out, before we see the big car of His Lordship's make a dust towards the ranch.

The car came to a stop by the corral where us boys had been busy; His Lordship clambered out and he was packing a grin the likes of which we never thought we'd see on a face like his, and then he says:

"Howdy, boys!" That was another surprise. And he went on before we had a chance to return his greeting:

"I've brought a couple of friends which I'm sure you will all be glad to see again, and I want to present them to you according to their position. This gentleman," he says as he opens the back door of the car, "is the new superintendent of the Y-Bench, Mr. Saunders, and this young man is Mr. Buttons, who has consented to take his former job as the horse-wrangler for the same company."

His Lordship stepped to one side, and there a-grinning from ear to ear stood our old cow-foreman, who'd been let go when His Lordship had took it onto hisself to handle the outfit; and beside our old foreman, who now was promoted to superintendent, stood "the kid," our little horse-wrangler.

To see them all a-standing there, along with realizing what their presence meant, was sure a surprise to us — more so with the transformed features of His Lordship.

We all stood around sort of paralyzed for a spell, and then Bearpaw took the lead, and we shook hands all around, His Lordship included, and for the first time.

"The Y-Bench has had a very narrow escape," says His Lordship as we all gathered at the bunkhouse that night, "all due to my inexperience, and I am very grateful to you boys for what you done to save it. From now on I'm willing to resign as cow-foreman and be only the interested owner, and if Bearpaw here will take the position I tried but failed to fill, I would be very pleased."

Bearpaw stood up and spoke.

"And I'd be mighty pleased to accept, Mr. ——" He stopped.

"My name is Montgomery," says His Lordship, "and I would like to have that remembered by all of you."

"All right, Monty," says Bearpaw, grinning.

And from then on His Lordship was always spoke to and as "Monty," on the Y-Bench range.

SILVER-MOUNTED

IV

"HOWDY!" We turned at the voice of a stranger who, outside and setting on a good-looking bay horse, was looking at us through the camp's only window, and smiling.

Strangers was mighty scarce in that country, and mighty welcome; and when Long Tom, our foreman, returned that stranger's "howdy," it was natural-like followed with "Turn your horse loose and come on in."

It was a while later when a shadow was throwed acrost the door and the stranger walked in, and still a-smiling begin unsnapping his bat-wing chaps.

"We just got in a few minutes ago," says Long Tom, "and the cooky's got 'er all ready. Go ahead and wash up; we'll wait for you."

The stranger had gone to the wash-bench outside, when Little Joe leaned my way and in a low voice asks: "Say, Bill, did you see the boots that *hombre's* wearing? And look at them chaps," he goes on while fingering of 'em. "Soft as silk, and with silver mountings."

I sure had noticed them boots; they was the kind any cowboy would glance at more than once. The flower design that was on 'em, in inlaid colored leather and bordered with many rows of fancy stitching, would attract a blind man. The soft kangaroo vamp, with the well shaped, not too high heel, sure had my eye too. The chaps was of gray soft leather, the wing covered with leather designs, and pure silver ornaments on the belt and more along the wing.

"It'd be a shame to use an outfit like that in this sunburnt lava and sage-brush country," says Joe. "It'd sure skin the pretty spots off it in no time."

The stranger, all washed and hair combed, walked in again, and all of us trailed over to the long table to partake of the last meal of the day. The talk was as usual, and not ruffled any by the presence of the stranger. Once in a while he'd inquire some about the country, and his talk fitted in well. Before the meal was over, and without asking any questions, we had him figgered out as a rider from the prairie countries, but we wasn't sure. A few days would tell, and we hoped he'd stick around, for we'd sort of took a liking to his ways, fancy outfit and all.

It was early the next morning when a few of us boys was at the corrals and rolling that day's first cigarettes. The *remuda* hadn't got in yet, and while waiting, we run acrost the stranger's rig. A real fancy saddle it was, all hand-carved and weighed down with silver, and on the "*rosaderos*" was letters saying: "*For First Prize in Bucking Contest.*"

Them carved letters sort of identified the stranger to us, but there was other things about the outfit that was a puzzle and which didn't match none at all. Like for instance, there was a real honest-to-God-well-made saddle with a neat little silver horn, bare and for tying, and instead of having the hard-twist grass rope coiled up on the side of that saddle, and which was the only kind that belonged there, there was a sixty-foot raw-hide *reata*, plumb useless, and not at all fitting with it nor the slick horn that was on it.

His bridle didn't agree no better; the head-stall belonged to Wyoming, the bit to Mexico, and the rawhide reins to the California Spanish. None ever go together, and it was sure a puzzle to us how that waddy worked or where he was from.

But we was soon to know. The *remuda* was being drove in the big corrals, and about that time we spots Long Tom coming down with the stranger. Our hopes that he'd stick around went up to the top as we seen the foreman pointing out a string of ponies for him to ride; and seeing it was settled that he was going to be with us for a spell, we all went after our ropes and begin snaring our ponies for that morning's ride.

Our ponies was all caught, saddled, and ready to "top off" when we see the stranger circling a rope over his head and try-ing to run the horse he wanted, with a "Missouri throw." He was using a braided cotton rope, the kind that's used in spin-ning, and we figgered the rawhide *reata* that was on his saddle was only for an ornament.

To begin with, we seen he was no roper, not while he was on the ground, anyway. Long Tom watched the proceedings of the whirling rope for quite a spell; he didn't want to tell the new hand not to whirl his rope in a corral full of horses, on ac-count he figgered the stranger ought to know that without being told, but he didn't like to see the ponies getting all jammed up and skinning their hips on the corral-poles, either. He was just about to flip his rope and catch the stranger's horse for him, when he stopped and seen that *hombre* do a funny thing. The stranger, after missing three or four throws in the "Missouri swipe" fashion, had coiled up his rope and built another loop; and instead of whirling it this time, he begin to spin it. He kept a-spinning it till the horse he wanted circled around the corral and came within roping distance, and about that time the spinning loop shot out, never losing its circle, and caught that pony under the chin, and then the loop settled over his ears.

Long Tom and all of us grinned, looked at one another and shook our heads. The throw the stranger had just made matched well with his fancy boots, chaps and saddle: it was fancy too. But it seemed like there was no end of puzzling things about that stranger, and the next to happen was after we'd topped off our ponies and all of us was ready to line out of the corral gate. I was somewhat surprised, after I made my horse quit sweeping the corral with his foretop, to see that the new hand hadn't saddled his horse yet; he was just a-hanging on to him, wondering what to do, and seemed like looking around for something he couldn't find. Finally, he looked at Long Tom, who was setting on his horse and waiting.

"Is there a chute I can saddle this horse in?" he asks.

The horse he'd caught was a spooky little sorrel and a fighter, and he wouldn't let the stranger come any closer than a safe ten feet from him. He wasn't the worst horse that outfit had, not by a long shot, but he wasn't the gentlest, either. The foreman sized the stranger up for a spell and finally says:

"We saddle our horses in the middle of the corral or anywheres we get 'em — *out here*."

I looked at Long Tom as he said them last two words, and had a hunch right then that he knowed what kind of a man he was talking to. That was more than the rest of us could figger out.

Having no time to waste, Long Tom got off his horse, walked over to the stranger and told him to get his saddle. While the stranger was gone, the foreman flipped the loose end of the rope around the spooky sorrel's front feet and hobbled him; then he reached for the saddle that'd been brought up, put it on the slick back and cinched 'er up.

We felt sort of sorry for the stranger as that went on, for we could see that he didn't know what to do with his hands, and he just sort of kept fidgeting around, careful not to look at any of us; but he brightened up some as Long Tom handed him the bridle-reins and told him, "It's up to you now."

The stranger seemed glad of it, and the way he climbed that pony showed he was aching to prove that he was some entitled to that fancy outfit of his.

It was when the little sorrel bogged his head and went after the stranger that we got another surprise, and which made the puzzle all the harder to figger out. The stranger had seemed at home from the time the horse side-winded out of his tracks, and it was then we understood how it was he brightened up when Long Tom handed him the reins and told him to go ahead. That boy could ride.

He reefed that pony and made a fool out of him as well as Little Joe could, and Joe was about the best rider in the outfit. It made a mighty pretty sight too, to watch that new hand ride on that fancy outfit. The silver was a-shining to the sun at every curve of the horse's body; the long hand-carved tapaderos, along with the wide wings of the rider's chaps, sort of made the movements of the horse and man mighty easy to watch; and even old bronc'-fighting Long Tom had to stand there like the rest of us and admire.

Finally the show was over, and a little too soon to suit us, but we figgered there'd be some more later, as that outfit sure had plenty of mean ponies. We all filed out of the corral, and the stranger amongst us, a-riding along like he was sure a credit to that outfit he was setting on.

We loped out of camp, Long Tom in the lead and never looking back. Three or four miles out, the ponies was brought down to a walk; the gait was kept to that for a mile or so, and into a long lope we went again. A knoll twelve miles or so from camp was reached, and there Long Tom "scattered the riders" different directions — two up a creek, two more over a ridge, and so on, till all the boys was scattered in fan shape to hunt and run in whatever horses was in that country.

The "Double O" was a horse outfit, and run over ten thousand head of the finest horses a man wants to see. It took a big range to run that many horses, and the proof that it was big and also good was by the kind of horses that was raised there. They showed they had all the chance in the world to develop and grow full size, and they was wild, as wild as any horse ever gets, and if it wasn't that they was corraled once or twice a year, they'd soon turn into renegades, for even as it was, it took a mighty good hand who knowed horses, and he had to be well

It made a mighty pretty sight too to watch that new hand ride on that fancy outfit.

mounted, before he could turn a bunch of them and bring 'em toward the corrals.

As Long Tom scattered the riders, I'm thinking that most every one of us wished to be "paired off" with the stranger: he was such a surprising cuss, and if he could sashay horses like he rode the sorrel, that'd sure be another show well worth watching.

Most of the riders rode away two by twos, till there was only me and Joe, the stranger and Long Tom left. Then the foreman spoke again.

"Bill," he says, "you, and you" (pointing to the stranger) "take Lone Mountain; and me and Joe here'll skirt around Rye Patch."

I grinned at Joe and rode away, the stranger for my pardner. We rode along a-talking of nothing in perticular and everything in general. I was wanting awful bad to get an inkling, so as to clear the puzzle he was to me and all of us, but no hinting would make him give any information, and it sure never came to me to come right out and ask him, 'cause you can never tell what a feller's hiding in his upper story or what he's trying to keep as *past*.

To sort of make him feel that I wasn't wanting him to talk on himself unless he wanted to, I turned the confab toward the present and says:

"You want to watch that sorrel you're riding; he ain't through with you yet, and is apt to bog his head and go after you just when you least expect or want him to. But," I says afterward, "I guess you don't mind that."

I expected him to grin at me in a way that'd show he wasn't caring what the sorrel done or when he done it, and there is where I got another surprise; for the stranger instead of grinning as any cowboy would at my remark, seemed to turn pale, and then I noticed how he wasn't setting straight up and free, as he had when first leaving the corral. He was setting close now, and with a short tight holt on the reins.

We skirted the foot of Lone Mountain and then wound our way up it; it was a steep and high old mountain and could always be depended on for a couple of bunches of wild, highland-loving ponies. We was half-way up, and I was keeping my eyes peeled to see the wild ones *first*, when on a ridge that run to the mountain, and away up, I spots the buckskin rump of one horse, and I figgers there's a bunch with him.

I stops my horse and points his whereabouts to the stranger and asks: "See that horse up there?"

"Yes," he says, and he was looking away to one side of where the buckskin was; he wasn't seeing him at all.

"Well — anyway," I says, "you keep about the middle of this mountain, and when I start the bunch, I'll head 'em down your way, and you can keep 'em going on down toward the flat."

"All right," he says.

"Dag-gone queer," I says to myself as I rode away. "He's a top hand in some things, and a pure greenhorn in others. Now, he's never hunted stock much, or he'd sure seen that horse up there; and then again, his acting scared on a horse he *knows* he can ride, sure is past me figgering out."

I manœuvered around till I got on the other side of the
bunch I'd spotted, and when I got to the right place, I showed
up sudden and fogged in on 'em so quick that them ponies just
got scared and flew straight away to where I wanted 'em to go
— they didn't have time to stop and parley on how would be
the best way to lose me; they just went.

There was about fifteen head in the bunch, and one "marker"
amongst 'em identified 'em as Double O horses. I camped on
their tail for a ways and till I made sure they was headed past
where the stranger should be; he'd keep 'em from doubling back
up the mountain, I figgered, and fog 'em on down to the flats
as I'd told him to.

Taking another look at the bunch so as to make sure of their
going straight down the mountain, I sat on one rein, brought
my running bronc' to a crowhopping standstill, and then made
him head back, up the mountain. There was another bunch I'd
spotted up there. I circled around and on up, losing no time,
'cause I wanted to get that second bunch and throw it with the
first so as I could help the stranger in case he needed it; but
realizing what a big head-start he had on me, I had no hopes
much of seeing him and the first bunch till I reached camp.

It took me quite a while to reach the top of that mountain;
it was steep and high, and I didn't want to rush my horse too
much on account of the run I figgered I'd have to make to get
that bunch in. I let him take a good breathing spell when the
top was reached, and while I uncinched my saddle and cooled
his back a little, I took a look down the flat away below me for
a sign of the dust the first bunch I'd started would be making.

I had a mighty good view of the country from up there; it all looked like a big map a-stretching with the edges petering out into atmosphere. I could see the fringe of cottonwoods by the camp we'd left that morning, and the creek a-shining in the sun, but in all that landscape I couldn't see no dust. I wondered if the stranger could of got his bunch to camp already and while I was climbing the mountain; it could happen easy enough, 'cause there was nothing slow about them ponies once you got after 'em, and then again that stranger was so surprising, he might be a wizard at running wild ponies.

I got on my bronc' and lined him out in a fast walk toward the other bunch. I didn't see no more chance of having the interesting company of the stranger, and I was sorry for that. Anyway, I kettled the other ponies from the right side and fogged 'em on down a long ridge that stretched away out on the flat. It was a fine place to run, and my horse was a-fighting his head to get in amongst the bunch that was raising the dust ahead of him. All was going fine and to order, and I figgered at that speed I'd be in camp in a short spell, when in the canyon to the left I sees a big dust and another bunch of running ponies. They was headed straight up the mountain and the opposite direction I was going, and then I got a glimpse of the buckskin horse, the one I'd first spotted, and then the marker, which told me plain that there was the bunch I'd turned over to the stranger.

"What t'hell, now!" I says as I rode off the edge of the ridge I was on and into the canyon. I was hoping to turn 'em and throw 'em in with my bunch. The next half a mile I covered was sure no bridle-path, and the speed I made it in went to show

The next half-mile I covered was sure no bridle-path.

what a dag-gone fool a feller can be when getting het up on the subject. I'd turned my horse off into a straight down run, and the little shelves of shale rock that was here and there was all that kept us from going down faster than we did.

But I got in the canyon before the bunch passed me, and that was the cause of my hurry, for if the bunch had ever got above me, I'd just as well waved my hat at 'em and let 'em go. I'd never been able to turn 'em.

As it was, they'd had to go through me to get away, and they'd been handled enough so they didn't try it. They turned, went down the canyon a ways; then, when the sides of the ridge wasn't so steep no more, I turned 'em once again and up on the ridge where the other bunch was still going strong and the right direction.

Both bunches'd had quite a bit of running; they wasn't so hard to handle no more, and I had no trouble much getting 'em all together. All was going fine once more; my bronc' had quit fighting his head and a-trying to get in amongst the horses; he was glad to just lope along behind a ways and just follow 'em.

I loosened up on the *mecate* (hair rope) reins and rolled me a cigarette; then it comes to me: "What's become of the stranger?"

I looked at the country around as I rode, but no sign of him was anywheres; then I looked at the bunch which was keeping ahead of me about a quarter of a mile, and running my eye over 'em, I thought I seen something a-shining to the sun and on one pony's back; something else was a-flapping on each side of him. And doing some tall wondering, I rode a little faster so as to have a closer look.

It was hard to make out through the dust, but as I looked on and squinted I finally made out the shape of a saddle; but what bothered me was them things a-shining on top. Then I come near kicking myself for forgetting and being so dumb: them shining things was *silver;* it was the stranger's saddle, and under it was the sorrel he'd rode so well in the corral that morning!

I stopped my horse as the thought came to me that somewheres was the stranger, afoot, and maybe with some bones broke; for when a rider sees a horse packing an empty saddle out on the range, it sure sets him to thinking. A man can petrify out there and never be found only maybe by coyotes or magpies. Fifteen or twenty miles is a long ways with a smashed-up leg.

Of course the stranger might be all right, I thought, but there's no telling where he may be laying and crippled from a fall. There was only one thing for me to do; I fogged in on my bunch and took 'em as fast as I could. Halfways in, I could see the dust of other bunches being brought in by other riders, and I turned my bunch to meet one of the closest.

Throwing my bunch in with 'em, I stopped just long enough to tell the two boys that was hazing 'em in that the stranger's horse was in the bunch I'd brought in and he was afoot somewheres. Then I headed on the back-trail to look for him.

I picked up his trail where I'd left him and followed it along a ways. I seen where he stopped his horse and waited for me to head the first bunch down his way. From there on, the tracks of his horse was far apart: he'd been running him and, as I figgered, taking after the bunch as they come.

I followed that trail for quite a while; it was doing a lot of zigzags, and I could see that the bunch was somehow getting away from him and back up the mountain; then of a sudden I seen a patch of tore-up ground. It'd been tore up by the hoofs of the little sorrel, and in the middle of that patch was something that made me get off my horse for a closer look. There, as pretty as you please, was the print of the stranger's body where he'd connected with mother earth and measured his length. The stranger had been throwed off.

That was hard for me to believe, but there, and right in front of me, was plain proof. I took another long look at the tore-up patch, then got on my horse and went to cutting for tracks which would tell me where the stranger went. One thing I was mighty glad for, and that was he wasn't hurt, and when I run onto the trail he'd left with them neat heels on them pretty boots of his, I could see he was walking straight up and not staggering any, far as I could make out.

His trail crossed a creek, and there I felt better some more, for he'd had water anyway, in case he needed it. Acrost the creek, a few miles wide, many miles long and running toward camp, was a strip of lava rock. No earth was there to follow a trail, and I lost track of him, but I figgered he'd be following the lava strip back to camp, on account it might be a little easier walking there.

I rode on back toward camp following it, and feeling sure I'd run acrost him before he got in, but I rode many miles, and no stranger was seen. A little ways further, I spots the boys riding up; they'd started out looking for him too.

After I told 'em where I left his trail, they rode on to look for him; my horse was tired, and I went on into camp. The boys didn't get back till away after dark, and no sign of the stranger had been found. We built a big log fire by the camp that night and where it could be seen for miles around. It would burn a long time, and if the stranger was within ten miles, he couldn't fail but see it. We couldn't do no more.

The fire burned down; morning came, and still no sign of the stranger. Two riders was sent out to look for him that day, and when night come and they rode back, the disappearance of that *hombre* was still as much of a puzzle as ever. It seemed like the earth had just swallowed him. Another day went by, and it was as the mountains was throwing long shadows that Joe points out to a dust acrost the flats. A rider was making it.

The last horse had been unsaddled as the rider came up to the corral gate and got off his horse. It was the stranger, but a very different-looking stranger than he'd been a few days past and when he'd made his first appearance at the horse camp. There was a stub growth of whiskers and hollow cheeks on a face that'd been round and smooth, and the alkali dust that covered him from head to foot sure done the work of disfiguring all he'd been to look at.

We all greeted him as though nothing had happened, and not a question was asked; we didn't have to ask, on account that there was everything about him that told us all we cared to know and plainer than words. It was all easy reading, the same as the print he'd left in the foothills and where the sorrel throwed him off.

The horse he'd rode in wore the brand of a neighbor outfit which was some thirty miles away, and knowing he couldn't of caught him on the range with a saddle on him and all that way, it was easy to see he'd rambled on afoot for some time till he come to one of that neighbor outfit's camps, borrowed the horse, and got his directions to come back on from there. Yes sir, the stranger had went and got lost.

It was sure a mystery to us how a man that could ride like he'd rode the sorrel, and do such fancy roping as he'd done, could turn out to be such a freak. "How and where," we'd ask one another, "can a man learn to ride like he could, if it aint on the range?" Nobody could answer that, and the mystery instead of getting any clearer with reasoning, kept a-getting deeper.

The next day came, and a long ride was ahead for that morning. The stranger showed up at the corral and we seen him make his spinning loop with a lot of interest. That interest went up many notches as we seen that same loop settle around the head of a tall, rawboned brown horse. That horse was one of the meanest buckers in the outfit and didn't belong to his string none at all; but he'd mistook him, amongst the two hundred ponies, for one that'd been pointed out to him that first morning.

"I guess you don't want him," says Long Tom, riding up. "He ain't in your string, and besides, he's sure hell on wheels when it comes to bucking."

"Whose string is he in?" asks the stranger.

"Nobody's; we take turns at him once in a while, and he's for anybody that wants him."

"Well, I guess I'll try him, then, if I can get somebody to help me saddle him."

He got all the help he wanted, and in less time than it takes to tell it, the saddle and bridle was on the big horse, and the blindfold ready to take off soon as the stranger was well set. That *hombre* climbed on not a bit ruffled, and when ready, he told us so in a way that would make us put our money on him.

The blindfold was yanked off, and it was no more than done when the tall gelding called on his wiry frame to do its duty. Two spurred heels went up in the air about the time the horse did, and when that pony buried his head in the dirt in a hard-hitting jump, them spurred heels came down on his neck and played a ringing tattoo there.

Between the bellering of that horse, the ringing of the spur-rowels, the sound of that pony's hoofs hitting the earth — all a-popping, and keeping time — it sure made a sound worth sticking around for by itself; and even if a man couldn't of seen the goings-on, he could of told by them sounds that here was a hard horse to ride, and on top of him was a hard man to throw.

The stranger seemed in the height of his glory; he was setting up there, and fast and crooked as the jumps came, he wasn't caught napping at any of 'em. He met that pony halfways in all he done, and when finally the big gelding seemed to have enough and held his head up, we'd forgot that the man on top of h.m had let a little sorrel horse buck him off, we'd forgot that he'd let a bunch of horses get away from him on the range, and even his getting lost and roaming straight away from the home camp seemed away in the past. The stranger was one of us again.

We filed out of the corral and strung out on the morning's circle. Me and the stranger was riding side by side and by ourselves a ways; I expected that brown horse to go to bucking again most any time, and sure enough, Long Tom had no more than started us out in a lope, when I glimpses a brown hunk of horse-flesh transformed into a cloud-reaching and then earth-pounding whirlwind. I heard the beller of the pony, but I didn't hear no spurs ringing, and when I looked for the reason, I was surprised to see that them spurs wasn't at all where I thought they'd be — on the horse's neck. Instead of that they was buried in the cinch with a staying holt, and I thought for a second that I seen the stranger grabbing for the horn.

Little Joe, who'd been to one side a ways, rode close about that time, and I noticed the blank look on his face, like he didn't believe his eyes; and my face must of showed about the same look as I stared back at him, 'cause I know I was sure as surprised as he was.

Somehow I was glad when the brown horse quit bucking and lined out on a lope with the stranger *still* on him; I sort of hated to get disappointed in that feller, and I could see that Joe felt the same about it; but we both could see that it was pure luck the stranger hadn't been bucked off — he'd rode his horse like a rag and hung on with a death grip.

"That feller seems like a different man outside a corral," Joe remarked as we rode on, a-trying to figger out the puzzle.

Long Tom done a mighty fine job of scattering the riders that day; most every man wound up by hisself, and none of us got to see one another again till the circle was made and we was within a few miles of the corral wings. Every man had a bunch, and some two, and when the gate closed on the last bunch that was run in, we all natural-like begin to take a tally on one another, to see if any was missing.

It was then that Long Tom points at me and Joe and says: "You two better change horses; take an extra one along and go look for the stranger. I'm thinking he's afoot again." Yep, the stranger was amongst the missing once more!

It was pure luck when we found him, near sundown. Joe had spotted an object up on the ridge that first looked like a prospector's monument, and when we rode up on it, it turned out to be the stranger a-setting on his saddle. His clothes was near all tore off of him, and the fancy saddle looked like it'd run up against a buzz saw; it was all twisted out of shape and caked with dirt.

The stranger's spirit was sort of low too, but he managed to smile as he seen us, and half-hearted-like told us how the brown horse had bucked him off.

"But what happened to your saddle?" asks Joe.

"Well, I guess that's my fault," goes on the stranger. "I never figgered that a cinch gets loose as a horse runs and ga'nts up. I'd been running him up a slope and the saddle slipped back. After he bucked me off, it turned under his belly, and, as you see, that pony sure done a good job kicking it apart."

We all rode on back to camp, not saying much. I'd glance at the stranger once in a while, and I could see that feller was thinking about something mighty strong. I wished he'd let us in on his thoughts, but it wasn't till we'd near reached camp that he seemed to want to loosen up.

"I can't figger it out," he says.

"What's that?" asks Joe.

"Well," he goes on, "it's the difference in my riding, and why there is such a *big* difference between riding a bad horse out of a chute where there's a band playing and folks cheering, and riding that same horse out where there's not a soul for miles around. I seem to lose my confidence out here by myself this way; and then riding along, not knowing just when the horse is apt to go to bucking, sort of gets on my nerve. I've come to find out that it sure ain't like riding that horse in front of the grand-stand. I *know* he's going to buck there, and exactly when. I'm prepared for it, and when he's through, I'm through riding him too.

"You notice," he says after a while, "that I ride very different when inside of the corral than I do when out of it. . . . I guess that only goes to prove I'm a show-hand, and not a cowboy. I followed circuses and Wild West shows as a kid, and learned to ride there. Afterward I took on contests, but I never rode a bucking horse outside of corrals or show-grounds before. I don't have to tell you that I never rode outside of town limits either — you can see that; but it's sure surprising to me how much there's to contend with out here, not only with the kind of horses a feller rides, but the country is so daggone big, and there's so much a man has to know, to work in it and qualify."

We was saddling up as usual the next morning when we notice the stranger had picked his own horse. He tied a few belongings on the saddle and then turned toward us all as we was getting ready to file out for that day's riding.

"I'm not riding with the outfit to-day," he says, walking toward us and smiling. "And you boys wont have to look for me after the day's ride is over, 'cause I'm going back to where I can ride my bucking horse inside a fence, where there's people around to watch me, and a brass band playing and keeping time with my pony's hoofs as they hit the ground."

He started to get on his horse and ride away. We watched him the while and noticed what a change had come over the fancy rigging that'd been so pretty and shiny just a few days past. The neat boots was et up with alkali, the fancy stitching all unravelled, from the ramblings he'd done afoot. The saddle was all loose and tore apart here and there.

"The country sure put its mark on that outfit," says Joe as we rode out of the corral. "Dang shame, too; it was sure pretty."

A month went by, and then one day Long Tom received a letter from the stranger; inside the envelope was a newspaper clipping and telling some of the winners of the prizes at some rodeo. Heading the list was a name underlined; the man packing that name had won first prize in the bucking horse contest and first in rope-spinning also. At the bottom of the strip was handwriting which said: "The name underlined is yours truly, *the stranger.*"

We all read the strip; after which Long Tom poured a little syrup on the back of it and pasted it to the wall. On the top of the strip, and to sort of decorate and identify, he nailed a twisted piece of silver which the brown horse had kicked off the stranger's saddle. It had been found that day out on the hardpan flat.

THE LAST CATCH

V

I'D been at Sand Wash camp for near a week before I noticed that up on one of the high ridges and hiding amongst the junipers, sunning themselves, was a bunch of wild ponies. They was backed up against a high rocky ledge which not only sheltered 'em from the cold spring winds but reflected the heat of the sun on 'em.

Then again it was a fine place for 'em to doze and sun themselves on account that the only thing that could very well get up there was mountain goats; they was safe enough from mustang runners, and if any ever did ride toward 'em they could always see 'em first.

I'd noticed how they'd be at that spot near every morning when the sun shined, and also noticed their tracks where they come to water at night, a mile or so above my camp. — An old corral was up there and showed, the way it was built, that it was a mustang trap at one time, many had been caught in it I could see, and when the mustangs was thick, but now it was down in spots and I noticed it'd been neglected for quite a spell.

The water came out of a spring right inside of that corral and sunk in the ground a few feet away, still inside, and that's where that little wild bunch was watering.

My mustang-running fever raised up again when I thought how easy I could trap that bunch by just fixing up that corral and close the gate on 'em as they came in. I'd run and caught many a wild horse and still remembered the thrill, but now I was punching cows for a big outfit once again, had a steady job, lots of good bronc's, good camp and good grub — and I tried to forget mustangs and how easy it'd be for me to catch that little wild bunch that was up on that ridge, but they was always up there reminding; I felt the wild-horse fever getting me and I was trying hard to keep it down.

And most likely I could of kept it down too, only, one day I happened to get a closer view of the black stallion that was in that bunch and the mustang fever had a hold of me once more — I wanted that black horse, I never stopped to think *why*, but I wanted him.

The days was long, and after my day's ride was over I'd go to the corral and try to fix it up so it'd hold the black horse and his bunch. I was mighty careful in the fixing too, on account that a too big a change in the corral would be noticed by the mustangs and if they got suspicious they'd go and water somewhere else.

But with a few live junipers and pinons with the branches and all still on, I managed to make everything look natural, and strong enough to hold any wild horse. — In a few days I was ready, fresh tracks showed that the mustangs came in to water as usual every night, and one night I took my stand by the trap and waited.

It was along about the middle of the night when I heard the wild bunch coming up the sandy wash, the sound they made brought back many memories and my heart was thumping again. Right on up they came and acted like they would walk right into

One day I happened to get a closer view of the stallion that was with that bunch and the mustang fever had a hold of me once more.

the corral without any hesitating. That would be too easy, I thought — but there they stopped and bunched. I could tell by the snorts they was suspecting that all wasn't well, but as nothing stirred and all seemed as usual, they finally lined in.

I could make out the outline of the black horse as he stood with head up while his bunch was drinking, that long heavy mane, curved neck, and pointed ears was easy identified. All was inside and I was about ready to pull the rope that'd close the gate when, for no reason that I could see, the band stampeded and scattered out like a bunch of quail a-snorting and shying. I could near touch some of 'em, so close they passed by.

I figgered right there that my chances for catching the black horse that night was gone, but he hadn't drank yet and maybe he'd come back. He was out there with his bunch and I could hear him nicker, the same as to ask if everything was all right as he scouted around 'em. — Then when all got quiet once again and I kept a-waiting, I finally heard a horse coming; pretty soon I could make out a black shape, the stallion was coming in to have his drink, alone.

That's just what I wanted — the black stallion alone, for I didn't care for any of the rest — and when he put his head down to drink I pulled on the rope and closed the big pole-gate with a bang.

I couldn't sleep very well the rest of that night on account of wanting to see that black at close view and with the sun a-shining on him, the first light of day found me awake and waiting for it. A hunk of pitch pine soon had the little stove a-roaring, the coffee pot begin to sing and by the time I'd went and caught me a saddle-horse and came back, the coffee was boiling; a cup of that and a cigarette and I was riding up the wash toward the trap corral and the black horse.

I'd no more than got sight of the top poles of that corral when a long whistle and a snort told me he was still there, and as I rode up I found a quivering picture of horseflesh that was sure good to look at, and that's all I did for a while was look; the more I looked though, the less I liked the idea of putting a rope around that black shining neck, for sometimes a rope sure does take the hair off in spots.

But I was too excited just then to worry about what a rope could do to a horse that fought it, and as I kept a-watching and admiring every move that black was making, and noticing the deep heart, the short back, and the long sloping hip that was some of his good points, I was natural-like uncoiling my rope, and making a loop.

He fought like a wild-cat when that loop settled over his head and drawed up back of his ears, but I was riding my best rope-horse that day and, with the brand new rope I'd saved for such a purpose tied hard and fast to the saddle-horn, I knowed I had him for keeps. Being careful of keeping the slack out of the rope, so as none of us would get tangled up in it too much, I edged my horse toward the corral gate and opened it —. I was going to take him to another corral close to my camp.

The distance to that corral, with the black horse pulling on the rope for all he was worth, was sure covered plenty quick, but when he got sight of the new corral, he started another direction from there and I had to do considerable manœuvring to get him

The distance from the trap to the corral was covered in no time.

through the gate and into it. Next was to put the hackamore on him and tie him up.

I'd planned to start breaking him right away, but I wanted to take my time at it and do a good job, and as luck would have it, cattle begin scattering and straying away right about then, my time was all took up with 'em and I'd hardly ever get back to camp till away after sundown. As it was, the only chance I had to see my black horse was early in the morning and before I started out for a day's ride.

Things went on like that for quite a few days, and then I begin to notice something wrong, the black horse was ganting up pretty bad, wouldn't eat and wouldn't drink and I was getting worried. I'd give him plenty of fresh hay and even turned him loose in the corral, thinking it'd help, but all that attention didn't seem to better things any with him; the only thing that seemed the same was his spirit, he'd show plenty of that every time I walked in the corral, but there again I could see what kept that up. I'd often caught him looking up toward that big rocky ledge where him and his little bunch used to sun themselves — and that finally got to working on me.

I'd think of that often as I rode along through the day and somehow the more I thought on the subject the less satisfaction I was getting out of the idea that I'd caught the horse and had him in my corral, all safe for whenever I wanted him. And then soon enough I realized —, it wasn't owning the wild horse that made me want to go after him so much, it was the catching of him that caused a feller to get the mustang fever, and after the mustang was caught and the fever cooled down — well, I'd kinda wished they'd got away.

I'd quit running the wild horse on that account, and here I was with another one I'd just trapped and took the freedom away from. I had more horses than I could use as it was and what would I do with this one, sell him? not hardly. I was too much married to them ponies I already owned and I knowed it'd be the same with the black horse, I'd never sell him even though I had no use for any more.

I'd been running them thoughts through my mind for quite a few days and had come to no conclusion, and every morning found me making tracks toward the corral where I'd smoke a cigarette and watch my black horse — the hay I'd give him would hardly be touched.

Then one morning I started the fire as usual, put on the coffee pot and walked out toward the corral. I figgered on coming back before the fire died down, but as I set by the corral I forgot everything but the little horse there with me and the country around us. All was quiet excepting for a meadow-lark tuning up on a juniper close by. I felt like just setting there breathing in and listening — and I was thinking, thinking as I watched the black horse. He was standing still as a statue and looking up where his little bunch of mares and colts used to be at this time of the day. Finally I stood up, took in every line of him, like for the last time, and then I leaned against the corral gate and opened it slow and steady and *wide*.

The black horse seen the opening, and maybe it's a good thing he took advantage of it right then, for a minute afterward I felt like kicking myself for letting such a horse go; but that feeling didn't last long and instead, it done me good to watch him pace away, head and tail up, and seemed, like hating to touch the ground for fear another trap would spring up and circle him once more. Then, as I watched him disappear out of sight, I felt relieved — Somehow, he was better to look at that way.

The coffee had boiled over, put out the fire, and scattered grounds all over the stove when I got back to camp, but I felt sorta cheerful and whistled a tune as I rebuilt the fire and put on fresh coffee.

A few days later I tore down the mustang corral by the spring and snaked the posts away with my saddle-horse. Then one morning I seen the black stallion and his bunch again; they was up by the big rocky ledge and just a-sunning themselves.

TWO OLD TIMERS

VI

"YESSIR, the country is all shot to pieces, the range is all gone, the cowboys have turned farmers, and the white-faced muley cow, which to me looks like a cross between a hog and a rhinoceros, has took the place of the wild-eyed range critter we used to know."

Old Dan Whitney was talking on his favorite subject again. It was a subject he more than liked to hark back on, on account that it all had been his life. He'd been born and raised in the cow country, and the fortune he was now having the benefit of had come from range cattle and the holdings he'd fought for while a cowman.

He'd been a king at the hard game, made his pile while the making was good and happened to sell out at the right time, which was when the "doped-up" homesteader begin to fence up the land, and before the first clouds of the World War appeared on the skyline.

In the years that followed, after Old Whitney had turned the deed over and changed his home grounds from the long rambling log house on the river bottom to a Spanish style "dobie" mansion on a California beach, that old cowboy had turned his back to the cow country for good, he didn't feel able to stand the sight of what he *thought* had happened there; instead, he'd let his imagination exterminate the big range world till he'd figgered every part of it was cut up into ten acre plots with a fenced-in farmer on each.

He'd took it for granted that when he left the cow country the range cow had disappeared too and he could near see the plough and wire fences swarm over where all that critter had roamed. Then prohibition came in and that, he thought, sure put a cap on things. He'd settled back in his comfortable chair more satisfied than ever that he'd quit just in time and before the country was too far gone. He *pictured* the cowboys with a glass of soda pop on one hand and a hoe in the other.

"Yessir, the range country is sure all shot to pieces," he remarked once more to the man setting near him. He waved a hand at the big stretch of ocean which could be viewed from the porch, "and now I'm thankful" he went on "that I can at least depend on *that* never being fenced."

The other man looked at the long straight line where ocean and sky met, and grinned. Frank Baldwin understood. He was an old timer too and felt the same and all what Old Dan kept a ruminating on.

Him and Dan had been neighbors when neighbors was forty miles and more apart, when, as they liked to keep a saying, it was "just the Government and us." They'd rode side by side from the time the long-horned cattle begin to take the place of the buffalo, fought side by side when the sheepman came, afterward, and tried to graze his blatting woollies on their range. They'd stuck it out together through blizzards and droughts, and won out in spite of everything.

Yep, they'd fought the injun, the cattle-rustler, and the sheepman, and even with all that fighting they'd enjoyed the life; it was *free* and they was fighting with a chance to win, the big odds

Him and Dan had been neighbors when neighbors was forty miles and more apart.

against 'em had made it all the more worth while. But when the railroads begin to come, and branch out here and there, was when the two cowboys had sort of felt a pinching at the throat. Pretty soon there was plenty of wagon tracks to be seen; them wagon tracks had branched out both ways from the iron trails and was scattering out on their range, bringing settlers. Then it wasn't long when the first strands of barb wire begin to make their stand and a few years later that barb wire had accumulated till it sort of formed an entanglement and trap which threatened to cut the cowmen's throats. There was no fighting chance no more.

The range that Dan and Frank had blazed a trail to and which they'd stood up for was gradually took away from 'em by the homesteaders. The big flat benches which was fit for nothing but cattle and horses was soon fenced up; so was the creek bottoms, and when the two old timers begin to gather up their scattering cattle they found many dead alongside some homesteader's fence. The fences had kept the stock from drifting in to shelter and out of the sting of the blizzards.

But that wasn't all; cattle had been killed by them same homesteaders and carcasses of fine steers was found where they'd been butchered only for one hind quarter, — the rest would be left to waste and the cayotes.

After a lot of hard riding going through a lot of fences, following lanes and opening many gates, the two old timers finally got their cattle off what once was free government range onto what was left of their leases and other holdings; then one evening Old Dan heard a queer chug-chugging noise coming up the creek and opening the door of the old ranch house he saw a buggy on the road. The old cowboy couldn't believe his eyes when he seen that buggy moving right along without any horses pulling it, but somehow he kind of figgered the noise that rig was making was what took the place of the horses.

Cattle had been killed by them same homesteaders, and carcasses of fine steers was found where they'd been butchered only for one hind quarter.

It was the first automobile in that country. Old Dan watched the queer rig work its way on up to the house and to a stop, then two slick-looking *hombres* in long dusters got out and smiled their way on up to the door and where Old Dan was standing.

It was the first automobile in that country.

The old cowman had his suspicions of what these two gents was, the minute they got out of the horseless rig; they was land-boosters. A few words was exchanged and then it dawned on Old Dan that they was out to buy his land and cattle.

That was agreeable to Dan, he was more than ready to sell. He set a price and the two men went chugging away, remarking that the price was too steep but that they'd think it over. They thought it over two or three different times and made as many trips, and each time Old Dan raised his price five thousand more.

"And it'll keep on being five thousand more every time you

come and inquire about it," Old Dan had warned 'em, "so if you want this layout you'd better decide on it mighty quick."

So that's how come that the deal was put through mighty sudden one day. And when the final settlement come and all the cattle and land was accounted for, one of the gents remarked that they got the layout mighty cheap at that.

"We're going to build a farming center right here," says that *hombre*, "and make millions out of cutting this all into small farms and a town site; in another two years you'll see this country in waving grain fields and supporting happy families."

"That sounds all right," says Old Dan. "But I'll bet if anybody gets any riches or happiness out of farming this land, it wont be the families."

It didn't take Old Dan many days to make ready to leave the old spread. He hated to leave Old Frank behind and have him see the country get tore up. but. as Frank said, "he'd soon be leaving too."

Old Dan spent his last night with a few of his riders at an old cow-camp, and his last words as he left the next morning was that soon as they'd turned over all the cattle, to "for god's sake hit out for a country where it'll never be farmed, — line out for the desert where the water is far apart and scarce."

It was a year or so later when Frank, Old Dan's neighbor, sold out and joined his partner to stargaze acrost the big stretch of ocean and imagine it all as prairie and range land instead of water. Old Frank brought stories with him as to what'd happened to the country since Dan left. A town had sure enough went up,

Old Dan spent his last night with a few of his riders at an old cow camp.

and right where the old home ranch used to be, and the whole country around it had been cut up in small patches and plowed and sowed.

"Has anything started to grow yet?" asks Dan.

"Not yet, maybe I wasn't there long enough."

"And you never would be there long enough," Old Dan went on, "that's not a farming country, it's a cow country. They think they can dry-farm that land but I know better; I know they'll need water to irrigate with before they can make it pay."

But four and five years went by and the news from the old range was that the new town was still "boosting" and that the farmers was still plowing up the soil and putting in their crops, and, even though there was no news of any big crops ever being harvested, the two old cowmen had come to finally think that they'd been wrong, that the old range country had sure enough agreed with the farmer and was giving returns for the tilling.

So, as it was, the two old timers gradually resigned themselves to thinking that the cow country had passed away the day they left it. They'd figgered that all the land of the cowboy, from Texas to Canada, had gone under in the same way as they'd seen theirs go under. Near every day the newspapers told of some new land that'd been opened to flocking homesteaders all over the West; then once in a while a whole sheet of the paper would tell of a new big dam gone up which would redeem the desert for miles around; truck farms and gardens would flourish where the bleached skull of a critter once told of awful droughts that'd parched that same land, and the pictures of 'before and after" of other projects of the same kind was enough proof of the success of stored waters and irrigation.

One success brought on others, more dams kept a-going up and redeeming more land, and then one day Old Dan called Frank over and showed him a sheet of newspaper on which was spread great plans to irrigate the whole Southwest. The two old timers studied the map for a long time, they spotted old range lands they used to know and which all was in the territory the big irrigating projects would take.

"But that might not go through for many years," says Old Frank, "and by that time we'll most likely be a-riding amongst the stars."

"True enough," agrees Old Dan, "but I'm sort of wondering about the younger fellers, the boys that used to ride for us for instance; they was too much cowboys not to feel bad at their country going out from under 'em."

But time took care of all that, time and happenings. The big war claimed many of the riders, and them that came back, having a taste of a different life to the one they'd been used to, sort of changed a little. Most of 'em of course went back to the range and appreciated that life more than ever before, and the others? Well, they wanted to fool around a little before going back. Contests and rodeos begin to sprout up here and there, and that sort of suited them few pretty well. The money they won at them events at steer roping, bull dogging, and bronk-riding kept 'em up respectable and all, with a high ambition to ride and rope for. Following them contests through the country, many of 'em wound up in California, where such doings are put on in grand style.

Once in that State, the movies begin to attract many of the boys; a few made good and a few others made just good wages. That's the way the whole thing layed, about the time the two old timers was worrying of what would become of the younger riders.

They knowed some of how things was with them riders, but they imagined a lot more. With all of what the papers, the magazines and books had to say about the old West, free range, and cattle being gone, it was no more than natural that they thought of the cowboy as being turned either into a farmer, a contest rider, or a movie actor, and they never stopped to think one minute that they themselves and other retired old timers like them was responsible for most of the rumors that the West and the cowboys was of the past and done gone.

Many a writer hunting up western material had visited Old Dan and Frank and rode the range with 'em *on the front porch of the dobie house*, it was such a comfortable way to find out *all* about the West, and it saved time.

The material they'd get from the two old timers would be of what them two thought or imagined had happened to the cow country since they left it many years past. They was like any other old timer, as old timers always was and always will be. The great times to any man are the times when he's got the gumption to try and make a go of things, and when that gumption fades away and a go of things has been made, a comfortable chair is hunted up, the fighting days are over, and, glancing back, the old timer remarks, "them was the times."

That was the way with Old Dan and Frank, their "times" was past and it had been easy for them to believe how when *they* left

the cow country that country went to pieces; they'd seen some
of it go with their own eyes, and with all they was reading about
dams, irrigation, redeeming, etc. that was enough proof to them
that all the land of the cowboy had went under the plowman's
furrow. And that's how come that when the writer out for western
stuff come to question Old Dan, that he'd be heard to say:

"Yessir! the range country is all shot to pieces, the range
critter is now dehorned and in the dairy barn, and the cowboy has
turned farmer."

The big wide porch of the dobie house was where many a remark of that kind had been passed about the cow country and the
cowboy, and the two old timers had been sincere in what they
said. If they hadn't meant it they'd still been on their range
and with their cattle, and believing, as they did, that all of that
was gone forever is why they'd left and sort of hid away in the
coast hills as a last retreat. They could live comfortable there,
the wide ocean sort of give the open feeling of the big range they'd
left and it'd never be fenced; then again, no neighbors could get
very close to them, so they thought, — the hills was too steep
and rough.

The two old timers spent their time reading the papers and
discussing all that appeared in 'em. With that and talking of old
times, and along with having a visitor once in a while, who'd always be called on to give his point of view on what all had stumped
'em, they'd managed to keep every day pretty well filled with new
interest. They'd been near contented.

They'd enjoyed squinting at the ocean and imagine things.
Between their mansion and that big stretch of water was a road

which when they first come had reminded 'em of the little old road that followed the creek bottom at the old home ranch; it was a wood road and travelled mostly by Mexican wood cutters, teams, and burro trains. That all looked pretty good to the old timers and it sort of helped to make their retreat to their liking.

Then one day, a couple of years after they'd settled on the coast, Old Dan, looking down the winding road from his porch, spotted one of these horseless buggies, a kin of the same that'd chugged up to the home ranch and which had packed the land boosters. Old Dan had called Frank over and, pointing at the rig, he'd remarked:

"I'd been hoping them things would never get this way," he says, then he went on, "I don't know how you feel about the sight of 'em, Frank, but to me they look sort of threatening."

The rig coughed on past their house and out of sight up the wood road. Two weeks later another one was spotted, then a week after that Old Dan seen three of them carriages, one right behind the other. From then on the horseless buggies seemed to multiply, and came a time when the two old timers didn't have to mark the calendar to know when Sunday come; the honk and engine clatter of the rigs told 'em a plenty of that day. It was the day when the crowds from the neighboring towns came out to picnic and bathe on the fine beach that was all along below the wood road and right in front of the old timers' retreat.

Then one day a road gang came up with teams and scrapers and in a few weeks had graded the old wood road to a good width; from then on the cars (they was called cars by then) swarmed along there and not only on Sundays but on week days also.

The old timers was told afterward that the road had been opened from one big town to another, and that accounted for the traffic.

The Mexican wood haulers' teams and burro trains gradually disappeared and big jarring trucks begin to take their place in hauling the juniper and pine from the mountains to the towns. Old Dan begin to feel another pinch at the throat, and as the gasoline smell and noise and all it meant got to the old timer's brain, he'd got to setting awful quiet and low in his chair, and his vision was kept to the line where ocean and sky met, above and past the steady stream of automobiles on the road below.

It was as the old cowman's imagination was performing the act of bringing a long winding trail herd of steers over the big ocean stretch one day that he was jarred out of his vision by the sound of a motor, louder, and strange from the many others he'd heard, and seeming like coming from some hard to locate direction. Old Dan straightened up in his chair, looked at the road below him, and, making sure that that new noise didn't come from there, begin to look other directions; then he spotted a big shadow a-skimmering along on the ground, like the shadow of some unbelievable big, bird and, looking up to see what was making it, he found hisself staring at another of man's creations, an airship.

Old Dan stared at the thing for a long time and till the strange ship, after making a big circle over the ocean, went back over the coast hills and out of sight. Frank had been inside of the house, showing the new cook how to make "hucky-dummy" and "son-of-a-gun-in-the-sack," and it'd never come to Dan's mind to call him to witness what he'd just seen.

But it wasn't many days when Frank himself spotted, not only one but two of the big birds, and when he pointed 'em out to Dan, that old boy just grinned kind of hopeless-like and then grunted.

Like the automobile, the airships got gradually numerous, so numerous that at one time Old Frank counted close to fifty of 'em in the air at once; they was army ships in formation, and in training to do their share in the World War.

The news of that war and all it meant was plenty awful enough to make the old men feel mighty lucky to be where they was for the time, without resenting the hand of progress that was steady creeping up on 'em. They felt lucky, not because they wasn't in the fight themselves but because they was away from the sight of suffering families and wounded men. They'd already done *their* fighting, plenty of it and for a good cause, and now that them days was over with 'em they only was thankful that they was away from the suffering that went with war, they couldn't of helped.

By the time the war was over the two old timers near got used to the automobile and tried their best to accept 'em in a way they figgered they should, but it was hard, if not impossible, to get out of their mind that them same automobiles was responsible and at the bottom of all the crowding they felt, and for that reason they sure couldn't very well fall in love with the rig.

The style and size of them things kept a-changing and went from high- to low wheeled, long snouted things; they also kept accumulating and bringing people out of the country of the old timers, by the hundred.

Then one day a bunch of carpenters and laborers set up a camp to within a hundred yards of the old timers' front porch. In three months a stucco house was up and before the new neighbors moved in, the foundation of another house had been started. By the time the rainy season come half a dozen houses, more or less the same style, and a-trying to imitate the Spanish with stucco and lath instead of adobe, had went up, and the windows of them kept a-staring at the old timers in a way that sure disturbed 'em.

But, regardless of that, progress kept a-spreading all over and around their retreat. Signs went up telling about choice lots, and two of them, in big letters and awful striking, was set up on each side of their place, a few feet away. By that time, gas, electricity, water, and sewer systems was all set in and the whole hillside plum down to the ocean was cut into lots, with a flag waving on each and telling of the name of the outfit that handled them.

With all that commotion going on, Old Dan begin to look up how much land he owned around his mansion, just to see how close any neighbor could get to him, and he found that, even though his land spread up the hill many yards back of the house, the front of it and the big porch was barely on his own territory, and it was as the rainy season was near over that one of the signs nearest his house was took down, the ground tore up, and a foundation started, right smack bang against his house.

Old Dan had near the same feeling again as he did when the homesteader begin to flock on his range many years past, and taking what seemed like the right of living and breathing away from him.

"I don't know," Old Dan says to Frank one night, "but it

strikes me like there's something wrong with our feelings and our ways of thinking. Now, these people that's building all around us, and flocking in like a bunch of bees, all seem so tickled the way things are progressing here. They're all doing their best to see that more flocks in and they seem to like it all the more if they're jammed up against a thousand neighbors, like a bunch of sardines.

"With us, and according to the way folks would think, we're like hermits. We don't like the rush, the noise, so many strangers and so close. I know it ain't that we don't like people, because we do, some; but I guess we like 'em best when they're scattered out a little, say about ten miles.

"Then," Old Dan went on, after a while, "there's progress and all it means, — I dont want to think that we're against that, and for that reason I wish I could get myself to liking and agreeing with all that's going on around here in that way. But I guess I'm getting too old and the change is too much."

"Well, it's a pretty deep problem," says Old Frank, shaking his head, "and I don't believe anybody but us and our kind could understand and figger it out. It's like our life on the range, Dan, nobody but us would live it. We was cut out for *that*, and I don't think none of us humans are cut out for more than one big thing in this world. We can't expect to be what we was, go through a whole life of that and then turn out afterward to agree with some other way of living that's teetotally different."

"And as for progress," Old Frank went on, "we done our share there. We and our kind blazed the trails, Dan, and started a mighty big industry in the cattle game. Before that industry was started, we was the kind that was in the lead of the soldiers when they went out of their forts to clear the land of Injuns on the rampage and make the country safe for the people that came.

"We done a lot in making the West peaceable and safe without the help of the soldier, and in more ways than one we're the ones that's blazed the trail for progress to follow up on, and then crowd us out afterward.

"Don't you never think that we are against progress, it's just that we don't fit into the times. We done ours and now it's past."

The summer came on and with it came the crowds to the beaches. The retreat of the old timers wasn't at all to be recognized no more as being the same where the two had come not so many years ago. New paved highways was being built all around the district, which now was called a "suburb." There was a steady noise of steam shovels, concrete mixers, hammering, — and mixing in was the honk of the big buses bringing buyers out to see "the new wonderful opportunities that was offered in home sites."

Then one day Old Dan, glancing at the landscape around him, and trying hard not to see it, noticed a big smoking hunk of machinery digging its way through the side of the hill and straight toward his house. It was a steam shovel taking cart loads of dirt at a time from the high side of the hill and dropping it on the low side. It was following the line mapped out for one of the new highways, and Old Dan's heart near went up his throat when he noticed that the stakes marking the upper side of that line went past to within a very few feet of the foundation of his porch.

Old Dan swallowed hard once more and let the thing come, that was all he could do.

The thing came on and kept a scooping big scoops of dirt from the high side of the hill to the low side. Pretty soon Old Dan felt the earth shaking under the house as the big machine came closer. On it came, day after day, and then one day, the grade was made past the house. When Old Dan and Frank went out to see "how they stood," they found a fifteen foot drop in front of their house, and so close that one of the steps leading up to the front porch hung on air, over a straight up and down dirt wall.

"Well," says Old Frank, a-trying to grin and bear it, "it looks like our front entrance is in the back now."

The big machine went on slow and finally out of sight; then came a time when the new highway was paved and opened to traffic. That was no more than done when, on the lower side of it and right acrost from Old Dan's, there sprung up another building, and alongside of that, right along that same highway, or boulevard, there went a string of shed-like contraptions, with partitions what looked like box stalls opening wide to the road. When the whole thing was done the first place put up one and ten signs about the merits of the gasoline that was sold there, and motoroils, etc. Then the other places hung out their shingles. There was soft drinks, hot dogs, barbecued meats, and all under one sign which said, "EATS." Another place, farther down the line, advertised the same thing to the passing motorists, with the word "grub." Then there was fruit stands whose owners was bound to flag the automobiles with their juicy fruits and loud hollers; but that wasn't all, there was a stall where baskets was sold, another filled with Navajo blankets, and right on down to stands of ripe olives, salted peanuts, and potato chips.

All that was, you might say, right under Old Dan's front porch, and facing a man who'd rode through the blizzards when there was no trails, when towns was hundreds of miles apart and when meals was on the hoof and only a well aimed slug could get 'em.

"Well, Frank," says Old Dan one night, as the echoes of the day's noise died down some. "It looks like the end of our string has been reached and our jumping off place has come. . . ."

One thing brought on many others to the booming community, and finally came a time, when cross streets run into the boulevard and were named, that Old Dan had to put a number on his place. Agents and peddlers of all kinds begin to swarm around, trying to sell anything from safety pins to oil wells; along with them came visitors to look at the old timer's mansion, just for ideas on the style of the Spanish; there was remarks of "how wonderful" at this and that, and if it hadn't been for Frank, Old Dan would of most likely give away most of the old Spanish furniture to sweet old ladies and nice old men who was "simply in love" with it.

Then one day Old Frank noticed a great big shining limousine winding around their place, seeming like looking for a way to get in. Finally the trail at the back was spotted and out of that limousine came a couple of slick looking *hombres* who smiled their way up to the back door. Old Frank looked at them in the same way somehow as a prospector in the desert looks at a circling buzzard overhead. There was something familiar about 'em.

Old Frank opened the door as they knocked, and it wasn't till they came in and when he shook their soft moist hands that it really came to him who they was. About that time the two gents smiled their surprise at meeting Old Frank again and said something about such being their good fortune and so on. Then Old Dan came in to see what was all the noise about.

"Well, well, well," they both said and smiled while meeting that old timer with open arms, and like he was a long lost brother, "this is indeed a pleasure."

The pleasure, it seemed like, was all theirs. If either Dan or Frank was pleased, they sure done a fine job hiding it. The old timers was surprised, of course, to see them two land-boosters away out on the Coast when, as they supposed, they was up in the north and having success in building a town and cutting up the land which would support so many happy families, the land that was once Dan's and Frank's cattle range.

It came to the old timers' minds to ask how the promising project panned out but they figgered it best to let them two show their hands, and after the howdedo was over, there was everything about the old men that went as much as to say, "Well, what do you want now?"

It seemed like what they'd first wanted, and the reason of the visit, was that they'd hoped to interest the owners of the mansion, which was Dan's, into a trade for some choice property in the same community. It would be a good trade, "you may be sure," and they wanted the mansion and the site it had only for speculation, but ——

"We had no idea it was you gentlemen who lived here," says

one of the visitors. "And as it is now," he went on, "I'm afraid a trade would be out of question on account that the property I would want to trade you for this one might be a little too modern to please you. It is a ——"

"Are you fellers connected with this land dealing and boosting that's been going on around here?" interrupts Old Dan.

"Why, yes. We bought this land some years ago, right after we cleaned up in your country, and we've been very successful with our scheme in turning this out as the fine residential district it is."

"Yes, and hot-dog stands," chips in Old Frank.

"But what's happened to our country up North?" Old Dan finally asks. "I expect you left a lot of happy self-supporting families up there."

"Well, we done pretty well there. That is we cleared up enough money to come down here and carry us through this deal in fine shape. Of course, the town we built was only to attract the settlers to buy our land, you know; it soon died after we left and most of the farmers have gone out of the country now. . . . Well, that country was only fit for cattle and horses anyway."

The look that came to the old timers' faces as they listened to the talk showed everything except pleasant. They might of carried near as bad a look during the days when sheepmen was found grazing woollies through the range they'd saved for wintering their cattle. Neither said a word, for words seemed useless. The two agents glanced at both Dan and Frank for a spell, then got up from their chairs, reached for their hats, and sneaked out the door toward their waiting limousine.

They drove away disappointed and scared, but they wasn't through with the old timers yet; they wanted that property awful bad, and somehow they was going to get it. They waited two weeks and till they figgered the old timers had sort of lost their hankering to commit murder, and then, to play safe, they wrote a letter and offering a price that was ten times as much as Old Dan had paid for the place.

Both Dan and Frank read the letter over careful, and sort of forgetting who it was from, Dan says: "Mighty tempting that price," and then he adds on —"but we're not after the money; all we want is a place to rest the last few years we've got left, and a little room."

"Yep," agreed Frank, "but room is getting mighty scarce out here now and this new boulevard out in front has doggone near dug us out."

"But where would we go?"

"Well, I don't know, but I been thinking since them boosters was here that it'd be sort of nice to see our old range once more and see what's really happened to it."

"That'd be fine, Frank, but I'm sort of leery of that. I got an awful blow there once and I don't believe I could stand another by the sight of what it might look like."

Weeks went by and the rainy season was near over when another offer was made to the old timers, by mail again. The letter wasn't even answered and as far as could be got out of 'em was that they sure wasn't figgering on selling, no time.

That seemed to be their intentions sure enough, but a strong hint came along and from the skies above, one night. It came along in the shape of a heavy rain which was more like a cloud-burst. The ground, all soaked and soft from the many rains before, was just waiting for that next downpour to start washing the scenery toward the ocean in fine style. The upper wall along the boulevard had started to crumble away pretty fast, and that night the two old timers was woke up by an awful roar. It seemed like the whole house had buckled up and give away, and when they straightened up to see what the commotion was all about, they found themselves staring out of their beds, right into open space.

The fifteen foot dirt wall into the boulevard had been washed out from under the front of the house, and the dobie wall of that mansion, having no support and being awful wet and heavy, just natural like followed the foundation right on down acrost the boulevard on toward the ocean and all escorted by a regular river of muddy water.

The two old timers set in their beds, neither saying a word, and by the early light of day watched part of their front porch a-skimmering along and on down. Then Old Dan spotted the chair which he'd set on so often, an old chair brought in from Mexico by the Spaniards, a century or two before. It was going on down in the muddy waters too, and making a last stand.

"I guess that's convincing enough," says Old Frank, after things had quieted down some. "We don't belong here, neither."

The next day, as the scrapers was clearing the muck off the boulevard and folks all around the community was estimating the damages of the storm, Old Dan was busy looking for a letter which he'd throwed somewheres a few days before. After quite a bit of looking around and with the help of Frank he finally found it, and the two together handled the pen and figgered out the words in answer to it.

They told of the conditions of the mansion, and that if the last offer still stood, they was ready to accept and close the dea at once.

A long Pullman train was pulling its way up a long desert wash to a low summit. It was headed north and east, mostly north. It was springtime, the sky was bright and the desert air was like wine, specially so to two old men who was setting out on the ob-servation-car and taking it in.

"Sure is intoxicating all right," Old Dan remarks.

Yep! it was the old timers a-setting there; they was headed back for their old home range, to give it a look, and hoping as they travelled that that look would do their tired hearts good. They'd felt pretty old as they'd been crowded out of their last retreat, and picturing the whole of the range countries to be all under fence and plowed and irrigated, as they had, didn't give 'em much ambition to be on the move. They'd only looked for more disappointment.

But as the train went on, the two old fellers begin to set up straighter in their chairs back there on the observation car. They was surprised that only a half a day's ride or so from the Coast was such open country as what they was seeing. Here, they'd thought, from all that'd been hinted in different ways, that this whole desert would be growing cocoanuts and pineapple by now, that the whole of it would be blooming with flowers, gardens, and

happy homes. But it was just the same, as it seemed, like it ever
was, and outside of the railroad track that went through the
land, the time could of just as well been the 1870's as the
1920's.

They passed Nevada and Utah, and even though the railroad
went through some mighty prosperous looking valleys and towns,
the old timers, with a knowing eye at the hills on both sides of the
valleys and beyond, could see that progress hadn't covered near so
much territory as they'd figgered. It had made considerable head-
way all right, but it was only in spots, and the territory that was
around, bare of any signs of any man's work, was still all range
land and awful big, so big that the spots where progress had
touched seemed, in comparison, to be very small specks.

There was many sights, as the train went on, that brought
sunshine to the old men's hearts. They was sights that no other
people on the long train ever noticed. Like for instance, twice
they'd glimpsed the white rumps of antelopes. The other passen-
gers never seen 'em and if they had, they'd thought it was white
rocks a-shining to the sun against the far away hillside. They
spotted bands of wild horses winding their way through the junipers and joshuas, and going to water. All that was plain reading
to the old timers. It told of many things, and it all spelled open
country.

By the time they reached the heart of Wyoming the old timers
seemed to've shed ten good years of their life. They'd begin to
do justice to all they paid for in the dining-car, and the porters'
and waiters' tips told some of the happy recklessness that'd took
holt of 'em.

"It seems to me like we been considerable hasty with our opinions, Dan," says Old Frank during their last day on the train, "why this country still looks like *home* to me."

"Well, you got to admit," answers Dan, "that things sure looked bad when we left, and anyway lets wait and see what's become of our range before we get our hopes up too high."

"Yes, but look at this," went on Frank, as he waved a hand at the big stretches of Wyoming rolling prairie all covered with good grass and with no interruptions of any kind for as far as the eye could see, "why, you know how we figgered that this had all gone under the plow, or dudes, and dude ranches."

The plow, sure enough, had never been there; it was part of the millions and millions of acres of the range country of the West where the farmer never stopped, — and, as for the dude ranches, they was huddled up in the northwest corner of that State, and the space them places took was only another speck, as compared with the big territory around that was still all cow country.

Late that night the train pulled up by a station in a little Montana town, and there the two old timers, tired but happy, got out. They'd come to the end of their trip.

They registered in the same old hotel that'd been their stopping place whenever they used to come to town to ship their cattle, and when they was showed to their room by a young feller who took their grips, they was pleased to see that it was their regular room whenever they came there. It hadn't changed, there was the bullet holes by the window, which told some of the days of the rustler war. Both Dan and Frank knowed the characters that'd done the shooting, they'd been more than present at the doings.

The next morning bright and early, the two old timers was up and sashaying around town, just to sort of see what'd happened to it. Quite a bit had happened to it, of course, but there was no mistaking it was the same town. They noticed two new hotels, streets paved, hitching racks gone, livery stables turned into garages, and so on; but there was many an old landmark that stood up for itself amongst all the new things.

Like the people, there was many that was strangers to 'em, but amongst 'em they could once in a while see the head of one they knowed well. Just the sight of them few meant a better welcome to the old timers than if the mayor and town-band had turned out to meet 'em.

On their way back to the hotel they stopped at the bank, and there, after the howdedo was over, the old president of the bank near prayed at Dan and Frank to take some of the land which had been on his hands ever since the farmers left the country.

Saying they'd consider doing that little thing later, the two headed for the depot, with intentions of buying a ticket to the town where the old home ranch had been, and there they got the surprise of their lives. They was told that that branch line wasn't running any more, that it hadn't been running for the past eight years, and, what was more, there was nothing left of the line but the grade, the tracks had been took off and the ties had been burned.

Old Dan turned at Frank at the news, they stared at one

another for a few seconds and then a big grin begin to spread on their features.

"What do you know about that?" says Old Dan, his eyes a-sparkling. "And they even took off the tracks."

They both got awful anxious to be at the place, all at once; there was only one quick way for them to get there and they took it. In half an hour they'd got a hold of a car and a driver, loaded the car with a little flour, bacon, blankets, and a few other things, and away it started on its forty mile trip to the deserted town and the old home ranch.

The road leading out of town was wide and gravelled, there was many automobiles on it, going both ways and like they was in an awful hurry to get there. On both sides of the road was farm after farm and house after house, none of 'em over a quarter of a mile apart. There was stores along that highway too, and gasoline stations, school houses, and high elevators for the farmers' grain.

The whole country sure looked prosperous and was, sure enough, a farming country, and the hearts of the old timers begin to beat sort of unnatural as mile after mile didn't seem to bring no change. The wide highway led on like a straight ribbon, flanked on both sides with green fields of alfalfa and new grain. It looked like there'd never be no end to it, for, as far as the old timers, whose eyes was a little dimmed by then, could see, it went on and on.

Then, after what seemed an awful long ways, the driver slowed down and turned to the left off the main highway, through more farms but not on as good a road. A high steel bridge was crossed and the old timers looked down at the wide river they'd knowed so well. Their cattle used to range near this far.

"The river is pretty low for this time of the year," remarked the driver, "and if we don't get much rain this summer the farmers are liable to run short of water to irrigate with."

So that was it, thought the old timers, these farms they'd passed was irrigated farms, and not the dry farms of the kind that'd tried to take over the range. It was a great relief for them to realize that and their hopes went up to the top once more.

Straight acrost the irrigated valley went the car, through a little farming town, and then it begin to go up a grade to the high benches where the irrigating waters couldn't reach. There was the dry farmers. Acrost the rolling land and for many miles around was shacks, each on a hundred and sixty acres or more and a-setting up there on the landscape, looking like something that'd just dropped from up above and landed there for no reason only for a place to land. Outside of the few shacks that was the closest to the little town that'd been just passed, the others seemed most all deserted, doors and windows closed, and the atmosphere in the dark inside, matched well with the rusty broken handle plow on the outside. It all was like a monument which told of hopes that came to life and then went under.

The car turned to the left a little and the road from then on was on the grade that'd been the railroad on which the train had hauled in more than it ever hauled out. It made a good road and all the driver had to watch out for was the spikes which had been scattered when the track was pulled up; them spikes wasn't good for tires.

The dry farmers' shacks kept a getting more and more scattered as mile after mile was covered; then came strips of open land which looked like they had been missed entirely by the soil tilling army, but, as the driver told 'em, them strips hadn't been missed, it was just that the shacks had been tore down when the farmer went away, and the fences had went too. Scattering over where oats and rye had once been planted was little bunches of cattle and horses, grazing on what was once again range land.

One more ridge and then Old Dan would be able to see where the old home ranch had been; he pictured the town that would be there instead and he sit tight, ready for whatever blow the sight might give. He was afraid to look, and it wasn't till he was sure the car was where he could get a good plain view of the land that he opened his eyes, — he wanted to get it all at once.

"Where's the town?" asks Old Frank to the driver.

"That's what's left of it," says the driver, pointing down the creek bottom, "most of the houses have been hauled away to the town we left this morning and for the farmers on the river."

Old Dan's heart went up ten notches at the sight he was seeing and the words he was hearing. His mouth opened to speak but he couldn't say a word, — he just looked and listened.

Outside of the few scattering shacks and run down fences that was left to mar the land, the old country still looked near the same. Even the old ranch house, which he thought gone to make room for town houses, was still there and looking like it was waiting for him. Part of his corrals was still up, and with the short time that old cowboy had to view his old range and home, he already pictured how, with a little hired help to pull away the fences and burn up the dilapidated shacks, he could make it all come back to life as the country he'd once knowed.

Yep! it would be even better than the country he once knowed; it would be *his* and not free government range for anybody to use. As his old friend at the bank told him, the land could be bought for very little more than a long lease would cost. He could get all he wanted and deeds for the whole, then he wouldn't have to contend with keeping the sheepman off of it and he wouldn't have to worry about straying herds of cattle or horses that'd take the feed away from his own stock.

All that went through the old man's brain as the car went on and finally came to a stop in front of the old ranch house. Here he got out and somehow he didn't look so much like an old man no more. He stood a minute and sized the old place up, and then, stepping on the porch, he looked the direction where the town's main street had once been. All there was to show of that now was a couple of houses on either side, but he didn't see them, they'd soon be going down.

The only inhabitant of the town was found when Old Dan, followed by Frank, walked into the old ranch house. He was a pack rat who'd made his nest of sticks and anything he could pack right in the middle of the floor of the main room. Outside of that mess to clean up, the old house wouldn't be needing much work done to it to make it as good as it ever was; it had sagged a little or maybe just settled, and it'd be good for many snows to come.

The two old timers was near like youngsters again as they took in what could be seen in their ramblings. The old ranch house and the country around brought many memories back to life again, and there was remarks passed such as, "Remember, Dan, when a few of us stood off a party of Sioux warriors, right over there by that cliff?" or, "remember one of the hard winters, Frank, when we couldn't see the high corrals for snow?" etc. etc. The two kept a-talking of the times each spot or other reminded 'em of till away late in the afternoon, and Dan was just in the thick of another of them old time happenings, when he stopped short and listened to a sound, like he wasn't believing his ears. It was a familiar sound, but he hadn't heard it for many years. It was the thump of boot heels on the wide porch and the ringing of spur rowels.

Old Dan jumped up and sticking his head around the corner of the house spotted a rider there; it was only a second later when the old cowboy and that rider sort of clinched into a handshake and happy cuss words. . . . That rider was none other than his old cow foreman who, regardless of Old Dan's advice to hit for the desert when the outfit "broke up," had stuck to the old home range. He'd been just riding by and spotting the car in front of the house, had stopped to say "howdy" to whoever might be there. Folks had been kinda scarce the last few years.

Old Dan found afterward that there'd been many others of his old riders what hadn't at all followed his advice in hitting for the dry country.

"It all makes me feel like a quitter," Old Dan remarked that evening to Frank and the cow foreman as the three was setting on the porch. "Here I pulled up stakes and left just when the country needed help most. . . . It's been under an awful spell, boys, but it came out through, all scarred but sure enough through and still alive, — now it's sleeping; the scars of the plow are healing and the dry weedy scabs are blowing away to the winds, the healthy skin of sod and buffalo grass is creeping up to make it all what it was, what it should of always been, and what it will always be, . . . range land."

Away off on the bench land the beller of a cow critter was heard, then a little while afterward that of a little calf answered. The skies turned from a sunset-purple to a deep blue, and then darkness, . . . the range land was resting.

COMPLETE

VII

IT all had been gradually shaping itself for months, but it didn't really come to a head, and "Dude" Douglas didn't feel no hint of it, much, till one night when as usual he was riding guard around the bedded herd. There's many things comes to a cowboy's mind at such times; the quiet of the night, the dark shadow of the big herd, and the steady swing of the pony's gait are all, it seems like, in cahoots to bring out what might be buried the deepest in a man's think-tank. And it was as that cowboy was riding along and sort of keeping his eye on the edge of the herd that particular night that the dark shadows of cattle and horns begin to sort of evaporate, and as what came to his mind took shape, there came visions like of a timbered hillside, then a creek with quakers and cottonwoods along it, and by them cottonwoods a rambling log house and corrals — his own log house and his own corrals.

Yep, Dude wanted a home; and when the first thoughts of that came to a head and hit him full force, he didn't, for some reason, want to think of what really caused the hankering for all that meant to jump up so sudden and so clear. He rode on around the herd, and at first laid it to the fact that it'd be awful nice to have a place to call his own, a good little bunch of cattle and horses bearing his own iron, and all the comforts such belongings would bring. He was tired of drifting.

But there was more to it than that; and to tell the truth, Dude

was trying to dodge what really was at the bottom of the sudden
hankering. If he'd back-tracked a little, he'd found that the
hankering had took root about the time he'd went to visit an old
friend of his who'd settled down and built a home amongst the
tall cottonwoods of Cow Creek. Dude had rode in from a long
ways to see him, and when after his tired horse had been turned
loose to a manger full of blue-joint, and with his friend he walked
into the house, — that was when Dude had sort of felt something
turn over at the back of his head.

He'd been met by his friend's smiling wife and little yellow-
maned youngster, and with the sight of them, the sound of their
voices, and all, with the atmosphere that was around 'em in the
neat kept home, Dude had felt awful lonesome all at once. The
peace and happiness he seen there had struck him as so great and
fine that he'd figgered it all to be only for a few of the luckiest —
and then, without Dude knowing it, was when the craving for
such really took root and begin to sprout.

And many months later when that sprout came to bloom and
caused that cowboy to vision a home in the shadow of the bedded
herd, it found him sort of riding light. He could get the place
easy enough, but it wouldn't be what a feller would call a home
unless it contained all of the same that his friend had, and there
was the stump. Dude didn't know no ladies; the few he'd met
was mighty scattering, and he'd been so took up with broncs
and ropes and critters, that he'd plumb forgot about 'em. That's
how come, when Dude was struck with the homing instinct, that
he sort of dodged the lady in the case. Ladies are mighty scarce
on cow outfits, and worse than that, they're totally absent. And

As a drifting cowboy, never no time did he get the easy end of the string.

in Dude's rambles, the few he'd met had only been at some shindig held at mighty scattering places during the winters, and his meetings with them went with very few words; it was mostly "how-d'ye-do" and "good-bye."

It wasn't that Dude didn't like the ladies nor that the ladies didn't like him, for the liking tallied away up and pretty well from both sides; it was just that that cowboy never stayed in one country long enough to ever get acquainted with the fair sex, real well, and even though the most of them he'd met had wished to see him a second time, spring would most always break up before then, and Dude'd most likely be on some new range five hundred miles or more away.

Dude's life, from the time he was a bit of a kid on his dad's range, had been all for a horse and a rope; nothing else had mattered excepting being a bronc'-rider "from away back," and roper to match. He'd took to that as natural as a duck takes to water, and inherited the twist of the wrist that made him an artist at a game that needs a lot of talent and something else; he had the nerve to go with it, and the size of him, which went well up above the average, was no hindrance. He made a mighty fine figure on a horse, and as the ladies would say "on the ground too," and the build of him made it seem like whatever he wore had just come out of the tailor shop.

"You could hang gunny sacks and canvas on that feller," it was remarked more than once, "and it'd look like creased serge."

It was from that that his nickname "Dude" had come; he always looked "dressed up."

From the Red Deer River up in Canada all the way down to

the Rio Grande on the Mexican border was Dude's territory; he'd been through all of it on horseback, and the thrill he'd get out of just seeing what it looked like on the other side of the hill had kept him on the move till his trail wound around and crisscrossed all through the big territory. If his horse got leg-weary or he come to some cow or horse outfit to his liking, he went to work for a few months or till his horse was rested. That way he'd rode for most of the biggest outfits of the cow country; and as a drifting cowboy, never no time did he get the easy end of the string; but Dude liked the rough end — no horse was too "goosy" for him, and no steer ever hit the end of the rope so hard that he didn't wish he'd hit it harder. If a rope popped or both horse and critter went down in a mix-up, it was all the more fun and agreeing to that cowboy's heartbeats.

Living the game as he was, and with his heart so deep in it, Dude had found no time for town and ladies. If he went to town it was only for a short spell; soon he'd want to lay a hand on wild quivering horseflesh, feel saddle-leather, and watch the loop of his rope settle over the horns of a bunch-quitting steer.

Dude was well along in his twenties before a change gradually came over him; that change was the cause of him losing some of his wild recklessness in his riding and roping. There came a time when that cowboy worked for one outfit for as long as six months straight (three months more than was usual for him), and then for the first time he begin to notice cows — that the critters was raised for beef and not only to rope; and the ponies he was riding — they was supposed to be used to handle the critters and not to be bucked out all the time.

If a rope popped, or both horse and critter went down in a mix-up, it was all the more fun and agreeing to that cowboy's heart-beats.

Of course Dude knowed all that from the time he was a little shaver, and he'd been a mighty fine cowhand even if he had been wild at it; but all he knowed about the handling of the cow and horse, and what for, had been sort of far-off facts and he hadn't worried about it. If his horse bogged his head and went to bucking while he was doing his work, it was a lot more fun than if that pony had just behaved hisself and all had went according.

But with the change that was steady crawling over that cowboy, happenings of that kind came to be further and further apart, and came a time when he was caught in the act of sure enough trying to keep his horse from bucking with him. Along about then, the cow foremen of the outfits he'd be riding for got so they could turn their back on that rider and feel that he wouldn't dab his rope on a critter unless it was plumb necessary.

Yes, Dude was getting serious. He'd turned his head from bucking ponies to guessing how much a steer weighed, and the rope on his saddle wasn't kept as well stretched as it used to. That cowboy's recklessness was making a last stand when he happened to drop in at his friend's place on Cow Creek, and along about then was when the last of it died proper. That friend had been a close second to Dude as a wild hand — the two had been mighty good pardners on that account, and neither one had any more to brag about than a good saddle apiece and a job. Now Dude's friend had a nice little spread and all that went to make a real home, while Dude still had only his saddle and his job.

Six good summer months had went by since Dude had visited his old friend on Cow Creek. In that time Dude had been with

one outfit steady, and with his recklessness gone, his ability as a
cow-man came to the top and was recognized, so that when fall
come he was "straw boss," with a hint from the superintendent
that he would have something better for him soon. His wages
had more than doubled, and Dude stayed on.

But about that time there'd come a hankering to Dude which
put the promised position as cow foreman on dimmer trails, but
he was glad of the bigger-paying job, because with it he'd be
able to realize his hankering sooner, and he'd sure be needing the
money to carry that through. In the meantime, he was careful to
save what he made — like for instance he wanted a new saddle,
as the one he had had lasted him a couple of years and it was
time for a new one, but he made the old one do him some more.
His pay checks of that winter and the summer before hadn't been
dug in much, and the numbers in his bank-book was beginning
to loom up.

Two summers went by, and Dude was still with the same outfit
and drawing cow-foreman wages; then, one fall, Dude told the
superintendent, if his job was still open after the winter was over
that he'd be back to take it. The superintendent said it would,
and Dude, changing his saddle from the back of the company
horse to the back of his own horse, rode out through the big gate
of the home ranch and headed acrost the wide open country.

It was a month later when a check was cashed in at the bank
which made the cashier look up that cowboy's account. There
was very little left of that account after the check was cashed —
maybe enough to buy a new pair of boots, but that was all.

But Dude wasn't worried about that; if anything, he was

happier than he'd ever knowed hisself to be for a long time. He'd just paid down on a place, not such a very big place, but a mighty good footholt for what more he'd add on later. It was the starting and foundation for all he'd hankered for, and set in a location that tallied up well with what his mind had pictured.

The place sloped from high timbered hills where fine logs could be skidded down easy; clear streams run down off them same hills to gather at the foot into a good-size creek; there was aspens and cottonwoods along the streams, and the land on both sides of that creek was rolling and covered with grass. Dude's footholt took in about two thousand acres of that land, but there was more adjoining which he would buy later; then as the place was "stocked up" there was State and private-owned land, which he could lease. All put together, there'd been no other place that could please Dude's drifting cowboy heart as well.

There was a comfortable log house already on the land, and it helped him considerable in his start, but after sizing it up careful, he soon begin looking around for another and better location for a house of his own building; this one wouldn't do, he thought, not for a home.

Then, to help things along, an old trapper came and stayed with Dude that winter. From that old timer he got a lot of help and pointers in cutting timber and setting it up for house logs — without that help Dude would of most likely found hisself up against it, because there was lots of things he didn't know about cutting timber and building houses, and his ambition to have and to hold might of dwindled down some.

As it was, everything went smooth as could be expected, and

there was only one thing which made him dodge a little once in a while; that was the remarks the old trapper would pass.

"I don't see what a lone wolf like you wants with such a big house as this one you're building," he would say, or, "You're sure finicky about the way these logs fit together — a feller would sure think you've got a bird for this cage, a long-haired pardner, eh, what?"

Dude would take it out on the logs when that kind of talk came up, and the chips would sure fly, but log after log kept a-being hoisted up and fitted neat at every corner and joint, and even though some sarcastic remark was bound to come every time a log with a little crook in it was turned down, Dude went on being particular, and seen that everything was done in a way that couldn't be bettered.

Through the winter and whenever the weather behaved, Dude kept at peeling and fitting logs. Christmas came along without his knowing it, and that day he was busy peeling more logs while the trapper went to follow his trap-line. After the four-room house was finished, there'd be a new stable to build, and corrals, and it would take many logs to do the work. Dude worked on like a beaver, and if the tunes he whistled or hummed all day along hinted anything as to his peace of mind, everything sure must of been agreeing in there and rubbing with the grain.

It was along about the time the ground hog comes out to look at his shadow that Dude backed away from his winter's work and called it well done. Outside of a little hardware and carpenter's fittings on doors and windows, the house was all finished, and it looked mighty fine.

The work was done with the help of his saddle horse, and that good big horse hadn't liked the job at first.

"Yep," says the old trapper, "but it seems to me like you ought to've at least located the bird first."

Dude left, and begin to get busy at dragging the logs he hadn't used toward where the new stable would be. That work was done with the help of his saddle horse, and that good big horse, even though he hadn't liked the job at first, had got settled down to it the same as the cowboy that was riding him had settled down to home building, something sure different to cowpunching.

The March winds was blowing acrost the benches when the stable was up, and the ground was thawing, so that the corrals could soon be built. Dude picked out the place for that and left the job to the trapper; the cowboy was due at the home ranch soon, and as the trapper had remarked that he'd like to stay on the place while Dude was gone, and tinker a bit that summer, it all made things mighty agreeable all around.

Dude rode away and felt mighty pleased as he topped a ridge and looked back. He took in the new buildings and his country around, and remarked as he headed on:

"I don't know what it's all going to amount to, but it's sure a fine start, anyway."

The old trapper was a great help to Dude that summer, and the finishing touches was put on in fine shape; and when Dude rode in that fall to say "howdy!" to the old timer, he got the surprise of his life at seeing his country full of beef cattle.

"Well," explained the trapper, who also savvied the cow, "I thought you might just as well get something for this good grass, and I don't think you'll snicker at the price I got, to let 'em graze here. And if you don't object," he went on, "I'd like to stay on here again this winter and do some more trapping."

"Sure, stay on all you want and see if that makes me sore," Dude grinned at him, "but being you're here, there's sure no use of me sticking around while I can draw good wages."

So, as it was, Dude went back to the outfit that winter; but when spring broke out, he told the superintendent that he was quitting, and quitting for good this time.

"I've got my own place now," he says, "and I'm going to start stocking it up this summer."

"Well, I sure hate to lose you," says the superintendent, "but I sure wish you luck; and don't forget, you can always draw top wages here whenever you want."

Dude was turning to leave, when the superintendent called him back. "Wait a minute," he says. "I want to give you a letter to a friend of mine at Miles who I know will help you stock your place up to any amount. You won't need the letter so much, because I've already talked my head off to him about you, but it'll introduce you anyway, and that's all you'll need."

Dude didn't head for his place as he left the ranch. Instead, he rode straight for town, and the frisky way his fresh horse lined out wasn't one jump ahead, no time, of the way the cowboy felt.

It was late in the night when he reached town, but early the next morning he was up and having a hard time to hold hisself down till the land-office opened, and when it finally did, Dude wasn't slow in getting to work. He applied for leases galore, till he figgered he had a plenty, and then all he had to do was to wait many days to see how much of the land he'd applied for could be got; it was expected that most of it was already leased, but anyway he'd most likely get enough, and while he was waiting to hear, he wasn't going to lose no time.

He no more than got out of the land-office when he headed for the whereabouts of the man he was packing a letter of introduction to. There, he was met at the door by a young lady that made Dude wonder to himself if he'd forgot to take his spurs off, and a glance at her smile made him wish he'd took time to invest in a town outfit and all. But Dude didn't pack that nickname of his for nothing — he passed over the ruffle a heap better than he could of ever knowed. Anyway, he was sort of glad, but not too glad, when a grizzle-haired straight upstanding old man she called her father came up to meet him.

Dave handed him the letter, and the old man's face more than lit up as he bellered out Dude's name and put out a hand for that cowboy to shake, and Dude noticed from the corner of his eye, as he was escorted away, that somehow the young lady didn't seem far behind her father in the welcome he was receiving.

It was an hour later when Dude stepped out of the house and started back for the main part of town. His small bootheels hit the hard sidewalks in a way that was all for high altitude, and there was a hint of a smile on his face that you see on a man when he has the world by the horns, with ten seconds ahead to beat the time record.

His trail was mighty clear. He could get all the money he wanted at a reasonable interest, and that way he could begin stocking up right away and start the ball a-rolling. It was no gamble; Dude was a cowman, and he seen where, with cold figuring, he could clear the mortgage on his cattle in a very few years.

He was humming a tune as he went and till he hit the main street, and then his far-away vision of hills and fat cattle was butted into by the sight of a well decorated window of a men's-furnishing store. Dude stopped in his tracks and looked at the display a spell; he had quite a bit to do in town yet, so he figured he'd just as well go in and invest a little and have it over with. He came out some time later with square bundles under each arm. Then he went to a hotel, took a room for a week and began to disguise himself to look like any town man.

Rigged up that way, he went to hunt up different folks who he was told owned land adjoining his place. It wasn't for lease but it could be bought, and that's what Dude wanted to do. With hunting up them folks and dickering with 'em, along with riding over to the stockyards once in a while to meet stockmen and sort of feel around as to where mixed stock could be bought and so on, Dude managed to keep pretty busy. The evenings was about the only time when he couldn't do much, and on that account he didn't like to see them come.

It was while Dude was strutting along during one of those long evenings and trying to kill time that he found hisself amongst a crowd of giggling couples; he seen 'em turn up a stairway where bright lights was shining, and music came to his ears. Dude liked music, and he stood at the bottom of the stairway for a spell, listening to it; then it came to him that he could go up if he wanted to — there was many others up there he could mix in with.

Dude went up, and he'd no more than got there when he was invited in by some *hombre* who said he'd introduce him to some dancing partners, being, as he'd took it, he was a stranger. Yep, it was a dance-hall and, well, Dude didn't mind.

The music was mighty fine, when it wasn't screeching, and the floor was kind of slick, but it wasn't bad; anyway, Dude took the first partner he was introduced to, and they went around the hall twice before he dared look at her. It'd been a long time since he'd been on a dancing floor, but he got along all right and the first try only called for another, and he took on new partners as fast as he was introduced to them.

Then, as the evening wore on, he found hisself dancing with one girl the second time. Before the evening was over he'd danced with her two more times, and as she left him at the end of the last dance, she said something about another dance being held some other place the next night.

Dude was there the next night; it all was some fun and it helped pass the time of evenings away. He danced with the same girl of the night before, again and often; she introduced him to many other girls, and Dude was getting popular, so popular, before the evening was over, that he was being missed the minute he sneaked away for a few puffs at a brown cigarette, and sometimes scolded.

A party was on, the next night, and the day after that being Sunday, a bunch was going to go on a trip to the mountains. They'd call for Dude at his hotel early in the morning, and when that morning came Dude was ready.

The cowboy had a lot of fun that day, fun along with experience, and he learned more about ladies during that trip than he'd ever learned in his life. He even got so he thought he really knowed a lot about 'em, and with that he got to watching his step; if he fed a potato chip to one, while setting in the touring car on the way back, he fed another potato chip to some other, and so on.

Parties, dances and the likes came pretty regular and Dude was taking 'em on as they come. It got so that he soon was acquainted with most of the young ladies of the town — he'd meet 'em on the streets as he'd be tending to his business, and when he'd come back to his hotel of evenings, there'd been several phone calls and there'd also be several messages.

But even with all that attention and entertainment, Dude was beginning to get restless. Two weeks had went by and he hadn't as yet received no word from the main land office about his application on the leases. He'd dickered for and bought more private owned land, and now that he was all done, he was aching to get out and look over some cattle and begin stocking up.

Finally, a few days later, the hotel clerk handed him a long yellow envelope. Dude looked at the letterhead and grinned, and he grinned some more when, on reading what it held, he found that he could get near two-thirds of the land he'd applied for. In a few minutes he had a check made out and sent, to pay for the leases, and half an hour afterward he was strutting out of the hotel, boot-heels doing double time.

But something he'd plumb forgot came to him as he stepped out of the door, and there he stopped short. He dug in his vest pocket and pulled out a well wore book — it was his tallybook, and mixed in among the brands and earmarks of cattle and horses was the names of many ladies; he'd made dates with most of them, and for some time to come, and now somehow or other he'd have to let 'em know he couldn't be there.

He came back in the hotel and went in the phone-booth and there he proceeded to call them up, one after another, and tell them that he was going out of town and that he couldn't be at this party or that shindig. He'd called up two, and it was taking a lot of time along with having to be firm and explain a whole lot, and even at that, it wasn't working so good. So, after Dude hung up on the second one, he thought of a better way — he came out of the phone-booth and went to the writing-desk. Writing was hard and sort of painful, but he could tell what he had to say, without being interrupted, that way, and when he was through he was through. The first letter was the hardest, but after that it went easier, because he only copied that first one till the last name was accounted for.

That summer was a mighty busy one for Dude. He was covering the country buying cattle, and sometimes, to get what he wanted, a deal would take him a hundred miles or more away from his place. He could only get there on horseback and in some of his scouting around he'd sometimes be gone for a month. Then was when he more than felt thankful that he had such as Bill (the trapper) to take care of the stock he'd already gathered, while he was gone.

Old Bill, it seemed like, had decided to make his home there, and he was using the old house that'd been already on the place, as his headquarters. One of the rooms was full of his traps, bottles of scent and bait, and plenty of furs always hung on the walls; then there was a corner full of ore samples he'd picked up in his rambles over the hills. If he'd decided to move, it'd took a good four-horse team to haul all he'd collected, but Bill seemed settled there to stay, and as Dude had remarked, that sure wasn't making him sore.

Old Bill would take to riding whenever Dude would leave the ranch to prospect for more cattle to add on to the herd he already had gathered, and that old timer never let nothing get away nor anything stray in. When summer come, it was old Bill who got a hay crew together and tended to the gathering of the feed, in case of a hard winter, and when Dude would ride in with a new-bought bunch of cattle, he always rode in with a smile at the way that old boy had handled things while he was gone.

When fall came and begin to color up the land, Dude had around six hundred head of cattle bearing his iron, also a nice string of saddle-horses. With that and the good country he had to range them on, that cowboy felt like he had all any man would ever want, and then some. He could settle down now and enjoy what he'd wanted most—his own cattle, horses, and place. As for the paying up of the mortgages on all of that, that didn't worry him any; he was cowman enough to know what could be expected from a bunch of stock that's well took care of, and as it was, when the first of the winter set in he felt awful contented with everything in general.

For the want of company, Dude took over and fixed hisself up a room in the same house with the old trapper that winter; things was more settled in the old house, and he could move in the new one when spring come. Old Bill didn't pass any remarks at that, and it made Dude wonder why he didn't, because there'd been the kind of a chance that old timer had always been quick at grabbing.

Winter started along in fine shape. Bill, being a top hand at cooking, took on that job, while Dude was glad to play flunky and wash the dishes, just so Bill would keep on a-cooking the way he could. The weather was averaging, and the stock, with all the feed and shelter there was around, got on fine; and every morning, whether it snowed or the sun shined, Dude was out riding through his cattle, keeping tab and taking care of 'em while Bill went out to his traps.

Bill and Dude got awful well acquainted that winter, and before spring come, there sort of formed a pardnership between the two that couldn't of been fazed with dynamite. They talked of many things, and while Dude couldn't dig in very deep in the older man's thoughts, that old timer got to know Dude better than Dude knowed hisself. Like a couple of times through the winter he'd caught the cowboy looking at his little tallybook, and he seen that it was names in there, and not brands and earmarks, that was the cause of him turning the pages. He also seen him put that book away while only a blank look showed on his face, like as if, after all, there was only brands and earmarks in there, and not the right kind.

All that was plain reading to Bill, the same as it was plain reading when one time, while looking out of a window over Dude's shoulder, Bill had remarked:

"I didn't know you could see your house from here, Dude. I thought all the time the trees hid it."

"Yeh, you can see a little of the roof," Dude had answered.

Old Bill had found Dude staring pretty often at that "little of the roof," and as the long wintry month of January came to an end, he begin to notice that the settled and contented feeling that'd been Dude's the first of the winter, was getting sort of undermined by a restlessness that gradually growed as the winter wore on.

That cowboy was taking more time with his cattle; he worked hard all day long and came in the house only when it was too dark to see; and from that, Bill took it that he was putting up a fight to keep his interest on what his heart had been set on, and Bill as usual was right. Dude *was* putting up a fight, and that cowboy was disappointed in hisself while fighting, and disappointed to find that the place, stock, and all, after getting it together, hadn't seemed to fill his hankering as well as he'd expected. The winter was hardly over and he already felt tied down with responsibilities, responsibilities that brought no returns, that is, not the kind of returns that'd make up for being free to roam.

"Maybe," he said to the winds one day, as he was riding along, "the interest is more in the getting, and not so much in the having."

But Dude hadn't hit the nail on the head when he said that; maybe he didn't want to, and maybe it was just that he was trying to dodge that kept him a-fighting and hanging on. Anyway, he hunted up all the hard work he could find and went at it like he was killing snakes. Some days he'd ride with Bill to the trap line, and that old feller kept the conversation going till there was no time for Dude to think on the side much, and being he was on the move, that helped considerable.

That was the way things went on with Dude till spring finally come along, and it didn't come along any too soon because, with the dreary gray days of winter, that cowboy's restlessness was getting the best of him, and he was already hankering for new country. The old roaming fever, which had been kept down by the thrill of going after something, was coming to life again, and that was a bad sign for Dude, for as a rule when the fever to roam begin to take holt on him, that cowboy just picked up and went.

He'd been in the same country for three years or so now, and that sure wasn't according to the way he used to be, and even though he'd changed considerable since, got more serious and less reckless, the hankering to be on the go still seemed strong in him. But with the coming of spring the flame to roam went down to a smudge, and Dude was glad. He was glad that the sight of the new little white-faced calves playing through the herd, his herd, kept him setting still on his horse and watching 'em. It would be hard to leave all this.

For a time, the visions of the new hills and new range of strange countries stayed in the background, and as the hills turned green and the cottonwoods leafed out, he rode his range and kept line on his cattle with near the same interest that'd been his while he'd worked and planned to get it all together.

The spring works kept him busy till well along in the summer. He run in a couple of broncs to break and teached them to hold the rope tight on the calves of his own herd while he was branding. There'd been over two hundred of the little fellers, and that put his herd up to around eight hundred.

July came along; and Old Bill, who'd been making steady trips to the hills and working at a "diggin," collecting more ore samples, told Dude that he'd ride line on his cattle if he wanted to go to town and take in the rodeo and doings that would be pulled off the fourth of that month.

Dude went in and attended the rodeo some. He also took his little tally book along, but most of the names had been erased off to make room for the brands and earmarks of his herd and new calves. Anyway, there was a few left, and Dude rang 'em up, just for fun. He found that most of 'em wasn't single ladies no more, but the few that was still single sort of made up for the others, and then he met a few more that he'd never seen before.

When, after a few days, Dude left town again, there was new names in that tally book, but as he rode his range and run acrost stray cattle or horses that riders might come to ask about, he was finding himself erasing one name after another to make room for brands which he'd mark down.

Only two names was left in that book when the fall winds and the first of winter came to chill the land, and when Old Bill, who by that time was beginning to drag out his traps again, would see Dude look through his tally book, he seen by that cowboy's expression that it was brands he was looking at in there, and not names no more.

From that, Old Bill got the idea that Dude had sort of resigned himself to what he had and that he would soon settle down, but after Dude took in his beef herd (it was a fine little herd too, and the price it brought him met all that was due for payment and then some), Bill noticed that he begin to get restless again—if anything, more restless than he'd been the year before.

The winter that came was a hard one; it was colder and there was more snow than there'd been for many a year, and Bill was glad. There'd be plenty of work for Dude to do, and the fight Dude would have to put up to pull his cattle through would tally up well with his spirits.

The blizzards howled on pretty regular till along about February, and Dude took the storms like they was nothing at all. He worked even more than necessary, and all would went well, maybe, only when February come, there came a strip of weather with it that brought Dude's fighting to an end, and his restlessness came to the top once more.

Old Bill stood it about a week and then suggested:

"Why don't you take a ride and go visit your friend over on Cow Creek? I'll take care of things while you're gone."

Dude grinned, saddled up his best horse and went, but it hadn't been a good idea, and Bill found that out a few days after Dude came back. He caught him often star-gazing around the house when he'd come in of evenings. The walls, with all kinds of clothes and things a-hanging here and there, the rough home made chairs and bunks, the table, and even the grub that was on it, was stared at in a vacant way.

"What the Sam Hill is the matter with you, anyway?" Bill asked one evening as he found Dude in one of his star-gazing spells.

Dude straightened up in his chair and grinned at the old timer.

"Daggoned if I know, Bill," he finally says. "I guess it's the rambling fever that's getting a holt on me again. Always had it and can't keep it down, and then again I feel sort of tied down, with this place here on my hands — I sure never thought it'd be this way."

"No, you're all wrong," Bill comes back at him. "It ain't the roaming fever and you're not tied down; it's just that this place ain't complete yet — that's it, not complete."

The old timer watched Dude for a while, sort of expecting a question as to what he'd meant, but it didn't look like there'd be any coming, and he walked away, leaving him plenty of chance to figger it all out by himself.

But there was no figgering much to do. The last visit Dude had made over to Cow Creek had showed him plain what was the matter; his friend had a *home*, while Dude had just a place, and as old Bill had said, "not complete." But Dude had dodged that fact, on account that he didn't want to feel that he was doing any figgering on the delicate subject; it'd spoil things and he'd wanted to get the place and let it transform itself into a home natural like and without his forcing it on.

When he got the place and built the new house, he hadn't even wanted to feel that he was preparing for anything in perticular, and now it begin to look like he sure enough hadn't. The house had been up for two years and there wasn't even a piece of furniture in it, and the little of the roof he could see from the window of where he was staying had sort of seemed like it was laughing at him. It hadn't worked out just right and Dude had got restless, he'd wanted to roam the same as before and with just a horse and saddle as his own.

One day Dude erased the last name out of his tally book and in its place a few brands of stray stock was jotted down. He'd rode away beyond the outskirts of his range that day, and away off in the distance a hundred miles or so, he seen the tall white peaks of mountains which he'd never seen before. The sight of them made him wonder what it'd be like on the other side, and for a while, as he held his horse still while his eyes followed the jagged line of the peaks, he near felt like riding on.

It got so that Dude didn't even try to keep that feeling down with work no more. Old Bill noticed it, and he wasn't at all surprised, one gloomy March day, to hear the cowboy begin to speak of new country.

"You know, Bill," he says, "come to think about it, there's a lot of country I ain't seen yet, and there's one perticular scope of it down along the border that I've always wanted to see. I've heard tell there's lots of wild cattle and horses down there ——"

"And if you wasn't tied to this place," Bill went on for him, "you could be there, ain't that it?"

"Yep, you've got it right," Dude grinned.

"Well, why don't you sell this place then and go to it?"

"The trouble is, I'm not so hankering to sell this place. I wish I could somehow keep it and ramble too."

"You can't do that," says Bill. "But I'll tell you what I'll do: if you're so rearing to go, I'll buy it from you if you want to sell it, and pay you what money you put in it. I'm not going to be cheated out of my home by your crazy rambling notions."

Dude looked at Bill kind of surprised, then laid a hand on his shoulder and grinned. "All right, Old timer," he says. "I'll think it over."

Dude thought it over for two days, and in that time he found it was one thing to think about doing a thing and altogether another when it come to really doing it. He liked the place more than he'd realized and even though it hadn't seemed "complete," it would be hard to get rid of. He cussed his rambling spirits for a spell but that didn't do no good, and at the end of the second day, Dude told Bill he was ready to turn the place over to him whenever he wanted it.

"All right," Bill spluttered. "Fine and dandy. But I'm telling you right now, that once the place is mine, it'll be mine, and never yours any more. You're too daggoned unreliable."

That was agreed on, and the next day, saddle-pockets filled to the brim with deeds and mortgages and all kinds of papers, Dude was on his top horse and headed for town. Bill was riding alongside of him and neither was saying a word. The last of the familiar country was left behind before Dude's spirits begin to perk up, and then a free feeling begin to take holt on the cowboy. He hadn't felt that way for a long time and when the first of it hit him, it was all he could do to keep from loping out, any old place, and letting out a war-whoop.

But the quiet way Bill was riding alongside of him hinted strong that that kind of show wouldn't be welcome much; and Dude kept the curb on his spirits, till it only showed on him a little by his talk of the southern country and other countries in between, which he hadn't seen.

Outside of a grunt or so once in a while, Bill kept pretty quiet, and it wasn't till the two had rode to within a few miles of town that the old timer said anything which sounded much like words.

The cause of his speaking then was the sight of a lone horse, to one side of the road.

"Looks like he's crippled, the way he's standing," says Bill. "And what's that object alongside of him, I wonder."

The thought of a hurt rider or horse made the two branch off and ride over to investigate, and as they got closer they made out that the object alongside the horse was a girl who was stooped down and seemed like rubbing the horse's ankle. She didn't see or hear the riders till the sound of jingling spurs came to her ears, and as she stood up and faced 'em Bill recognized his old friend's Ned Humphrey's pretty daughter.

Dude recognized her too. Ned Humphrey was the man who'd staked him the money to stock up his range with, and she'd been the girl who'd met him at the door that day when he came, to speak to her father, with a letter of introduction. Yep, he remembered her well, and when she looked first at Bill, then at him, he seen that she sure hadn't forgot and didn't hesitate none when she spoke his name.

Her horse had stepped on a nail on the road somewheres and went lame, too lame for anybody to ever want to ride him back. Dude got down off his horse and felt of her horse's hot ankle, but as he listened to the sound of her voice while she explained things, he somehow didn't hear a word she said, and, for a spell, he forgot all he knowed about horses and what to do when they stepped on a nail. He watched every move of her mouth as she spoke, and when she turned and faced him and asked him what could be done, the peek he got into the clear depth of her eyes didn't help him any, not as far as producing a sensible answer was concerned.

"I'll ride on in town," says Bill, coming to Dude's rescue, "and tell your father to send his car out for you. I'll send out some turpentine, too, so that when the nail is pulled out, Dude can doctor the horse up; then he can lead him on in for you."

With many thanks from the young lady, Old Bill rode away. There was a smile on his face as he put his horse into a lope and he was heard to mutter:

"I know Dude ain't the kind of a man to look at many a girl the way I seen him look at that one, just now."

And Dude wasn't. According to the way he felt, he'd never even seen a girl before, but he was sure making up for lost time, and as Bill rode away and the girl talked, Dude never broke in on the sound no time. His only trouble had been to keep the talk going, so he could listen and watch her, and to do that he had to chip in with his own voice, which to him sounded like a rasp against a buzzsaw.

With the coming of the car, which came considerable too soon, life stared Dude in the face again, and it left him stargazing and seeing nothing much. He was thinking — thinking hard.

"It's a hell of a note," he says finally. He spoke as if he'd been alone.

"It is really too bad," says the girl.

Dude looked at the girl surprised, then he seen she was looking at the horse's foot and where he'd also been stargazing.

"Oh, yes," he says. "Excuse me — the horse, yes, it is too bad."

But Dude hadn't been thinking about the horse, not at all. The car came and Dude, after doctoring the horse up in good

His only trouble had been to keep the talk going so he could listen and watch her.

shape, helped the girl to her seat, smiled and waved a hand as the
car started away, then stood in his tracks, hat off, and watched
the dust of it till it disappeared over the sky-line.

Somehow and sudden, the ailing, that Dude had been *wanting*
to call roaming fever, had died, and more than that, it was plumb
forgotten. The country he was riding in, while headed for town,

had seemed to take on new colors and he sort of wondered how it was he'd never before noticed what a good country it really was. Then his mind went back to his place and his spirits sunk away down at the thought of it. It wasn't his no more.

All of it had been turned over by, what he thought was, a fool notion to roam, and even though the deal wasn't put through yet, he'd agreed to it, and to him that was just the same as if papers had been signed and the money received. He couldn't renig.

Well, he'd just have to get another place, that's all; and Dude laughed. "And by golly," he says to his pony's cocked ears, "that one will be *complete.*" That is, he was pretty sure it'd be complete, and when he seen the girl that night as he brought her horse to her, he felt surer and surer that it would.

When Dude reached the hotel where he was to meet Bill, he found that that old timer hadn't registered there at all, but there was a note from him; it said that he had to take the first train out, to visit some relative who'd suddenly took sick and that he'd be back in a couple of days. There was a P. S. at the bottom which said that he wanted to close the deal soon as he could and for Dude to be sure and be there when he got back.

"Daggone the luck!" Dude says as he went to his room.

As far as the wait was concerned, Dude didn't mind that none at all. He was made mighty welcome at the Humphrey home and his time was well took up with the young lady there. Dude found no use for his tallybook for *that* stay in town. There was only one name and he didn't have to mark that one down to remember it, nor the phone number, either. He often walked to the Humphrey home without realizing he was walking and he could of found that place in his sleep, without one misstep.

There was only one thing aggravating him, and that was the loss of his place; he'd have a hard time finding another one like it. The two days went by when Bill was supposed to show up, and it wore on to a week, with still no sign of that old timer no-wheres.

Dude was happy but restless; he wanted to get the deal over with, so he could begin on another place, because by that time him and the young lady who he'd been keeping steady company with was already beginning to hint at some plans.

Then one day as Dude was in his room handing out a cussing at Old Bill for holding things up with his absence, a letter was slipped under the door. Dude, seeing it was from Bill, read the P.S. first. It was advice for Dude to forget his roaming fever and to try to settle down to staying on the place. Then Dude glanced through the other part of the letter and near had a fit at what he read. "On account of sickness in the family," it said (Dude didn't know Bill had any family), "I won't be able to buy your place, not for a while at least. In the meantime forget about selling the place."

Five minutes later Dude was up at the young lady's home and knocking at the door and it wasn't long after that when both him and her was seen coming out of that same door. Both wanted room and air, there was something mighty important for them to talk about, and as the two walked away, arm in arm, there was two grizzled heads watched them out of sight. One was none other than Old Bill's grinning features. He'd hid out as Humphrey's guest and from there had took in Dude's progress. The other was Ned Humphrey.

It was three months later when Old Bill, natural like as you please, overtook a wagon loaded down with picked furniture and hollered up at the whistling driver who was setting on the seat, manipulating the lines of his four-horse team.

"Hello, Dude!" he hollered. "Where are you headed for with all the load?"

Dude stopped his whistling, and when he recognized Bill a-setting there on his horse grinning up at him, he also stopped his team.

"Well, by golly, it's sure a surprise to see you," says Dude, reaching down and grabbing the old timer's hand. Then he squinted at him a second and asked: "I didn't expect you'd be wanting the place any more — do you?"

"No, no," says Old Bill, "I never did want your daggone place. All I wanted to do was to save it for you, 'cause I figgered you'd want it awful bad sometime." The old timer kept quiet for a spell and then went on: "But now, Dude, I wonder if you'd mind, if I holed up in the old house on your place as usual. You see, I kind of like it out there, and besides, I'd like to sort of putter around the diggin's I've got in those hills and set my trap-line there again next winter."

Old Bill never waited for an answer; a look at Dude's face was more than enough. He went on:

"What the Sam Hill have you got in that wagon? It sure don't look like a drifting cowboy's belongings to me."

"And it sure ain't," says Dude. "This is furniture; it's going in that new house." He laid a hand on his friend's shoulder. "That new house is going to be a home soon now, Bill — and complete."

THE BREED OF 'EM

VIII

"IF it wasn't that he'd be hard to replace, I'd fire that man, and mighty quick—" Such was the words that came to the chore-man's ears one evening as that feller was busy pumping the milk cows under the big shelter shed.

The San Jacinto ranch foreman was peeved, that much the chore-man could see at a glance, but there was more than that, he was aggravated by the fact that he couldn't do nothing to ease them peeved feelings of his. Here he was, foreman over twenty men and more, he had the privilege of firing any of 'em as he seen fit, but he was satisfied with his men, all excepting *one*, and that one sure made up for the others. He was aching to send him down the road a-talking to himself, but, as he'd said, it'd be hard to replace him, not only hard but near impossible.

He knowed that to keep making good as ranch foreman he had to have good men under him, men that understood their work, and the man he wanted to fire most was the best and steadiest man on the ranch. He needed him, and on that account he had to keep down his feelings, also keep the man that stirred 'em, and that's what hurt.

The foreman started to walk away from under the big shed, on toward the cook house, but he stood in his tracks as he seen the cause of his trouble come into sight and heading for the corrals. At a distance he sized him up with a long look; he took in the curved brim of the big hat, the tall straight slim built of the man on down to the neat-fitting high-heeled boots; then he turned and walked away talking.

"You'd think he was a king or something, the way he acts."

But if the foreman could of glimpsed into Todd Lander's heart as that cowboy went on toward the corrals, he'd found there just the opposite from high elevating kingly throbs. The cowboy was lonesome, more lonesome than he'd been for many a day, and all because he was by himself and the only one of his kind left on the old San Jacinto holdings.

He'd went to the corrals to see the ponies there and for the company they'd give. He was greeted by snorts as he climbed the corral poles and the wild ones scattered out to bunch on the far side; he'd just run 'em in off the range that day and they was pretty spooky. Todd set on the top pole of the corral and rolled a smoke while his eyes went over the slick rumps and backs of the horses. He savvied them, they fitted into his language.

He watched 'em for quite a spell, and his cigarette was over half smoked when the colors of the setting sun on the hills caught his attention, and then he found himself looking at the big range called the San Jacinto Mountains. They fitted into his language too. His dad had told him once, a long time ago, how come them mountains to get that name, but Todd had forgot that now, like he'd forgot many things that was while his dad was alive.

And, as his eyes left the mountains and far-away hills, to roam over the big fields and meadows that now strung out many miles both sides of the San Jacinto ranch, the cowboy thought maybe it was a good thing his dad was gone; he didn't think that the transformation, from open range and cattle to cut up fields of grain and alfalfa, as it was now, would please him.

Todd remembered when his dad was cow foreman of the San Jacinto. The fields he was not looking at was open range land then, and as a kid, by his dad's side, he'd chased his first steer, right on that same land where now tall stems of grain was waving to the breeze.

After his dad had gone, the San Jacinto changed hands, and with the new owner's coming there begin the disfiggering of the big range; the river that run thru the land was headed off by a big dam in a tall narrow canyon and the water was divided thru irrigating canals, in a way that'd cover thousands of acres. Cowboys drifted away, one by one, as grain fields took the place of range land; the thousands and thousands of cattle that went to make up the big herds of the San Jacinto was gradually sold, and dwindled away till finally there was only a few hundred left. Ranch hands with hob-nailed shoes had took the place of the cowboy with his stirrup-fitting boots, and the cow foreman was replaced by a ranch foreman who was a farming expert and imported from somewheres.

Todd had been the only cowboy to stay and maybe for no reason much only that this was the only country he knowed. He wasn't the kind that cared to drift much, and when the superintendent, a man who seemed to savvy cowboys, told him that the job of taking charge of the few cattle that was left was his as long as he wanted it, Todd had been pleased and he'd overlooked the fact that he had to ride thru a lane to get to where the cattle was running.

He ranged the cattle along the foothills of the San Jacinto Mountains and above where irrigation could reach. There was only around eight hundred head left and sometimes the herd would accumulate up to a thousand, a nice one-man job if all went well; but sometimes Todd had found himself wishing he was three men instead of one. Even at that, the cowboy smiled thru the worst of them times. It was his work and as a cowboy he done it all as it come, without a whimper.

There was many a raw cold day with a stiff wind blowing when he had to be in the saddle to eighteen and twenty hours at the time. The worst the weather was, the more he had to be out in it, but it was all in the day's riding and with no certain hours nor time to do it in. There was times, of course, along in the summer, when there wasn't so much work, but that was all due to his ability as a cowboy and his understanding of range and cattle. For long stretches, in good weather, he only rode two days out of three and very short hours even during the days he worked.

Them short days' work as they followed one another for a spell is what'd come to be the cause of that rumpus between Todd and the ranch foreman, or the farm boss, as the cowboy called him. The foreman had seen the cowboy ride in early in the afternoon, day after day, and how some days he didn't go out at all; he'd catch him in the blacksmith shop trying to forge out spurs and bits, and to the foreman that sure seemed a waste of company time.

He never stopped to think of the times when the bad weather kept the cowboy in the saddle from early in the morning, with nothing to eat thru the day and riding a tired horse, till away

Some nice day he would find the cowboy doing nothing much, only maybe tinkering around breaking a horse or fixing his saddle.

after the foreman had hit his bed and went to sleep. He never thought how when the cowboy rode in, even on the short days' rides, that he'd had no lunch hour and no lunch, and that he'd have to wait till night before he had anything to eat: that was a cowboy custom, and a custom that the foreman would of most likely disagreed with mighty strong.

The foreman only noticed the time the cowboy wasn't working during the regular hours, he didn't consider the time he'd worked away past them working-hours, and on that account he begin to fret when some nice day he would find the cowboy doing nothing much, only maybe tinkering around breaking a horse or fixing his saddle.

The day of the clash between the two came when the foreman met the cowboy heading back to the ranch early one afternoon. The rush of the haying season was on; ranch hands was scarce and the foreman was short-handed. When he seen the cowboy that day, it came to him to break the news to the rider, which would be that, after he was thru with his work from now on, to hitch up a team to a hay mower and finish up the day in the hay field.

The foreman broke the news all right, but they didn't seem to break well. The cowboy never looked at him and went to rolling a smoke as the foreman talked. His hat brim covered most of his face, and the foreman talked on about making use of his time and so on, till finally the cowboy looked at him from under his hat brim. His lips was near white as he held a match up to his cigarette and lit it.

He eyed the foreman for a spell, then, as tho he'd only stopped to roll a smoke, and just that, the cowboy reined his horse to a start and rode away. Somehow the foreman felt glad to see him go.

But as the afternoon wore on toward quitting time, the foreman gradually begin to get peeved; the cowboy and the mowing-machine wasn't showing up very fast. Quitting time came and still no sign of the cowboy on the machine nowheres. Then the foreman got really peeved. He was for firing that man right away, and he would of most likely done it, only it had struck him as he drove in that he didn't want to take the responsibilities of the cattle that cowboy had charge of. The ranch foreman didn't know anything about range and range cattle and cowboys, but, as he'd said to the chore-man that night, if it wasn't that he'd be hard to replace, he'd fire that man, and mighty quick.

As far as Todd was concerned, things was pretty well the same as before between him and the foreman, even from that day. Of course that's not saying much, because, to begin with, the cowboy had never noticed the foreman, not any to speak of. It was the same way with the ranch hands; he never noticed them either, only when they got in front of him. It wasn't that he didn't like 'em. It was just that they was of different breed and not the kind he was used to mixing with; they couldn't talk his language nor of the things he knowed.

To him, they was just part of a crowd, a happy-go-lucky crowd, and when he'd come in late of evenings from some long day's ride and gather with 'em at the big bunk house, he could sort of feel their eyes on him, as he pulled off his chaps, like as if he was something strange. One well meaning ranch hand sug-

gested one night as Todd came in late, that cowboys should form
a union and work regular hours the same as anybody.

Todd smiled at him and said: "There can't be no regular
hours for us. A cowboy can't quit snowbound or bogged cattle
on account of a meal or because it's quitting time."

Todd would lay in his bunk at night and listen to the talk of the
men. He'd sometimes compare it with the cowboys' talk and sub-
jects and found it a lot different. The ranch hands seldom ever
talked of their work of the day. Instead, it run to something they
was plum away from. They'd drift into politics or argue about
new mechanical inventions and predict things about this or that.
With the cowboys, the work of the day was pretty well gone over
by the evening fire, and the talk seldom went away from horses,
cattle, ropes, and saddles. There was pride in the work and how
each cowboy done it, and where there's pride there's always a
little jealousy. That way each man was contesting against the
other, each tried to be a better rider, roper, or cowman, and none
was of the same standing.

The working hours was never thought of, on account that with
them a man could show what he was made of. The kind of horses
he rode and how neat he throwed a rope all went for or against
him to tell what kind of a hand he was, and it kept him on the
jump, because no matter how good he might of been there is
always room for improvement in that game, and there could
always be somebody that was a little better.

Then in the evenings there'd be songs, old trail-herd songs that
some used to sing. There was even poetry at times, made right
there at the cowcamp. It'd always be about some cowboy and

some bad horse, and the whole outfit chipped in or suggested a word to make it up. Then sometimes that poetry would be illustrated too, for it seemed like there'd always been some cowboy around that could draw pretty well.

The talk, the songs and all went with the range — the cattle, horses, and the work. Todd missed that talk and them songs, and sometimes he felt a whole lot like hitting for some cow outfit. There was a big spread just the other side of the San Jacinto Mountains, that he knowed; it was still all open range over there and it would always be because there was no river to irrigate from, but as was said before, Todd wasn't of the drifting kind much. He knowed his horses here, and his cattle, and his range, and in a way he was satisfied.

The one-sided rumpus he'd had with the foreman didn't bother him none at all. He hadn't expected him to understand range work, and he'd been looking for a break to come sooner or later. Todd had forgot all about that when a month later, while riding thru a big pasture, the cowboy seen the foreman driving toward him. Todd noticed that there was more of a pleasant look on his face, as he stopped his team to within talking distance and pointed to a fence with his whip.

"That fence there," says the foreman, "has been tore down by your cattle, and I wish you'd find time to fix it before they get into the grain."

"Not *my* cattle," says Todd, also looking pleasant, "you mean the company's cattle, the same company you're working for, and as for fixing the fence, my dad left Texas on account he was asked to do that once."

The foreman drove away, peeved a second time. Todd sat on his horse, rolled a smoke and smiled. The foreman didn't see that the cattle had broke in from the outside fence which *he* was responsible for and was supposed to keep up, he didn't see that the cowboy would be busy till away after dark to get the cattle out of the big field and back on the range.

As it was, he drove away, and with intentions to get another man to put in the place of Todd soon as he could. He'd stood that cowboy long enough, he thought, but he never figgered that another cowboy, to qualify with Todd's job, wasn't apt to be the kind who'd get off his horse and do labor, either. To his way of thinking, any hired help should do as they're asked, and he didn't know that a cowboy, to be that, couldn't be a ranch hand too.

Todd rode on to his work, day after day, the same as usual and plum ignorant of the fact that the foreman was looking for another man to take his place. And as time went on, another thing happened which made the foreman want to fire Todd on the spot and without even considering.

The cowboy was at the ranch that day and topping off a bronk he'd started to break that summer. That pony had been loose for a long time and with the fat he was packing he'd got ornery and wild. Todd had to start breaking him pretty well all over again, and it was just as that cowboy was bringing that pony to time that it happened. The foreman had seen it all.

The bronk's orneriness had come to the top, and that pony, disappointed that he couldn't buck out from under the leather and cowboy that was on his back, begin to get sort of desperate and to looking for a way out. There was only one and that was the way he came in, thru the gate. Of course the gate was closed, but that didn't seem to matter much right then. Head down and bucking in grand style, the horse headed straight for it. There was a crash of timber as the eleven hundred pounds of wiry horseflesh hit it, and Todd, seeing that no timbers was left to knock him off the saddle, stuck to his seat and fanned his pony on out to the open.

It was an hour or so later when he rode back, unsaddled his bronk and turned him loose in the pasture. The foreman noticed by his watch that it was still an hour or more before quitting time, and seeing that Todd never even seemed to see the gate his horse had tore down, he thought to head him off and tell him about it.

Todd took on all the foreman had to say and then walked on to where he'd first been headed. Two days went by and the gate was still scattered splinters, with no sign of a new one taking its place. Then the foreman caught up with the cowboy once more.

"When are you going to fix the gate?" he asks, sort of peeved.

"When I hire out as a ranch hand," answers Todd.

For some reason or other the foreman had nothing to say to that. The answer had sort of crippled his tongue and took his breath away. He was mad, so mad that he couldn't say "you're fired," not as much as he wanted to.

He glared at the cowboy for a spell and walked away. He wouldn't have to say anything; he'd just make out a check for his time and get rid of him like he'd so often threatened to. He started to open the door of his office when the purr of a motor attracted his attention and a second later the big car of the superintendent

There was a crash of timber as the eleven hundred pounds of wiry horseflesh hit the gate.

[231]

came around the corner of the building and to a stop right in
front of the office.

The foreman was glad to see the superintendent at such a good
time, he'd tell him all about that cowboy and ask him to pick a
man to take his place, a man who was *willing to work*. The foreman opened the office door for the big boss and, doing his best to
hold down his feelings, begin to tell his story and all about that
cowboy who wouldn't do nothing but ride.

The superintendent listened for a spell and a grin begin to
spread on his features; then he held up a hand the same as to say
he'd heard enough.

"All the good cowboys that I know are that way," he says;
"if they wasn't they wouldn't be cowboys, for that's a deep game
all by itself." He kept quiet for a spell and then went on: "I'm
afraid it's my fault that you two have tangled and come to dis-
agree, and I am sorry for that too, because you're both mighty
fine men and I know you'd both get along fine under ordinary
circumstances, and what I should of told you before is this: that
Todd Lander is not working under your orders. I couldn't expect
you, being you're such a good ranch foreman, to also be a good
cow foreman, so I'd kind of figgered for Todd to be his own boss.

"I hope you haven't done anything that would cause him to
quit," sort of asked the superintendent.

"Well, if I have," says the foreman, "he sure don't seem to
worry about it."

"Good, because I'm very satisfied with him, so satisfied that
I am now buying three thousand head more cattle for him to
take charge of. We've got the range and we'd just as well use it.

Todd will be our cow foreman and with the riders he'll be needing I thought of making the Upper Creek ranch his headquarters. This is what I came to see you about and I wish you'd send a few men up there to fix the corrals and things that need fixing. Of course there's no rush about that, because the cattle I'm buying won't be delivered for some months, but do that whenever you can. In the meantime don't tell Todd anything about this, because I want to surprise him. I know it'll be *some* surprise."

Well, that sure put a different light on the subject, and as the superintendent drove away, there seemed to be a big aggravating load drop off the foreman's shoulders. There was a pleasant change on his face as he looked around trying to get sight of the man he'd once been so peeved at, but that man wasn't to be seen nowheres. He looked around the bunk house and most everywheres and couldn't find him, and he was just about to give up the hunt when he heard a crash of timbers that sounded like it come from the corrals.

That sounded like Todd, sure enough. When the foreman got there, he seen where a whole side of the corral had been tore down, and he spotted the cowboy a straddle the same bronk that'd made splinters of the gate a few days before. The pony was tearing the earth and wiping things up in long, high, and crooked jumps toward the open and unfenced.

The foreman stood in his tracks and watched the great and graceful ride that cowboy was putting up. He'd forgot about the corral and instead he was finding himself wondering how any man could stay on the back of a horse like that, let alone pulling off any fancy didos like that cowboy was doing. He stood still,

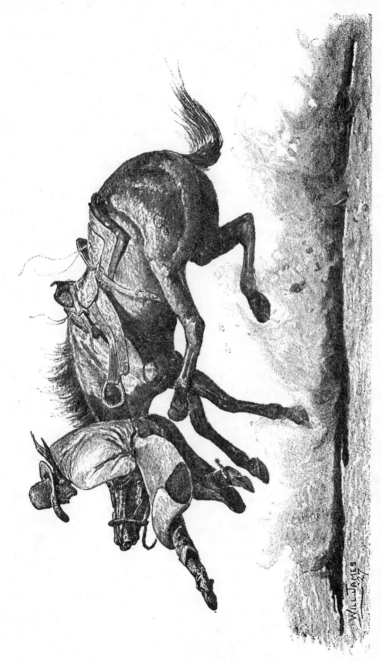

With the action of a cougar he slid out of his saddle and landed on his spurred heels out of reach of his bronk's hoofs.

watching every move of the man and horse, and for the first time, he really admired.

"You'd think he was a king or something," and this time there was no slur attached as the foreman passed the remark.

An hour or so later, when Todd hazed his bronk back to the corrals, he found the foreman there and waiting for him. The cowboy took in the damage his horse had done to the corral and he figgered that here would be another job that would be put up for him to do and which, as far as he was concerned, would be left undone.

"Looks like we need a new corral," says that cowboy as he twisted his bronk's ear. With the action of a cougar he slid out of his saddle and landed on his spurred heels, out of reach of his bronk's hoofs.

The foreman's eyes popped with wonder at the easy way the cowboy seemed to miss them flying hoofs, and, knowing horses, he also wondered how a man could handle, let alone ride, a horse like that, without having it in a steel-barred cage.

"Queer about this bronk," went on the cowboy as he pulled out the makings, to roll a smoke. "He seems to crave for open country the minute I get on him."

Todd had noticed a sort of different look on the foreman's face, when he first rode up. It wasn't the kind he'd ever seen there before, and he wondered about it, but he wondered a heap more when the foreman spoke.

"Well, I won't ask you to fix this, this time," he says, sort of grinning and pointing at the splintered part of the corral, "it wouldn't do me any good to ask you anyway — and what's more,

I want to kind of apologize for pestering you like I have, off and on, I ——"

"Hell, that's all right," Todd interrupted, smiling back at him, "I didn't mind it."

As the days went by, Todd wondered at what'd come over the foreman; that feller had turned from a glaring cuss to a friendly human, and the cowboy couldn't figger out why, but he had no way of knowing, and so, he quit wondering and accepted his friendship for what it was. Things went smooth from then on and Todd felt a lot more satisfied as he went to his work.

With fall coming on, the easy riding days of summer begin to disappear, there was no more two days' riding and one day's tinkering; there was more branding to be done, big calves to be weaned, and the cattle had to be shoved down off the high mountains before the heavy snows come. The cowboy rode out on a best horse early every morning and came in late every night.

Then, without warning, a howling blizzard struck the land, one of the worst blizzards the country had ever seen, and it'd come a month before any heavy snow could be expected. From then on Todd found no time to tinker around, he settled down to tall hard riding, and every morning, the same as tho the weather wasn't out of the ordinary, he rode out, faced the blinding storm to the highest peaks of the San Jacintos, and rode the high land for stock that instead of drifting to the foothills with the coming of the storm, had found shelter up there and huddled together while the snow drifted around 'em.

It was hard and ticklish riding getting up to them cattle, for it seemed like in no time the trails had been covered with fifteen-foot drifts, and the cowboy had to find a way around 'em, often putting his horse up rocky ledges that'd bother a human to climb. Then, the cattle that was left up there, being the wildest, wasn't what a feller would call easy to handle, specially in a country they knowed so well. Often they'd scatter like a bunch of antelope, at the sight of the rider, and hightail it any direction excepting the right one.

But no matter how wild they was nor how hard it was to get 'em down, the high country *had* to be cleaned of all the cattle that was there; the feed was all buried under the snow and on account of the drifts the cattle would never try to get down themselves, they would of lived on branches and twigs till finally they'd starve to death, *snowbound*.

The cowboy, knowing all that better than any one else, rode on thru the thick of the storm and made every minute count. He knowed that if the storm kept on he'd never be able to get up them mountains, no matter how he schemed or worked, and the thought of the hundred or more cattle that was still to be accounted for kept him going till it was impossible for him to go any more, and when finally he would turn back for the ranch, it was seldom that he was ready to quit, it would be his horse that made him turn back, for as big and powerful as his horse was, each one he'd ride out would be very tired and ganted up before he'd rein him toward the long trail to the ranch.

The tired horse of that day would then get a good rest, but there was no such a thing for the cowboy. He went on again early the next morning on another fresh horse, faced the stinging snow, broke trails thru the drifts and, by good manœuvring, persuaded the snowbound cattle to string out of their white walled prisons and follow the trail his horse had made.

There was times, on account of the snow being too deep, that the cattle wouldn't always follow them trails. The leaders would turn back, time after time, and then the cowboy would have to skirt around, ride his horse thru some other place, and make them another trail. All this work went on while the storm howled and the cowboy could only see a few feet in front of him. Sometimes he'd slide his horse into a drift that was a whole lot deeper than he'd thought. The horse would go near out of sight, then the cowboy would get out of the saddle, waller around, and by different schemes get his horse out.

That was mighty hard and muscle-straining work for both man and horse, and not only that, but mighty dangerous, because sometimes them drifts might be hanging over the edge of some ungodly steep place which, on account of the fast-drifting snow, couldn't be seen. A fall at such places meant only one thing, and the story of it would never be told till the thawing winds of the following spring took away the snows.

The storm kept up for many days and thru it all the cowboy kept in the saddle and breaking trails. Often the trail he'd made would be drifted over with fresh snow before he could get whatever snowbound cattle he'd found to follow it, then he'd have to ride ahead and break it over again. Every once in a while as he rode he kept a-reaching for a handful of snow and rubbing his face with it, but, even at that, the stinging frost had sneaked in and turned one side of his face white and then to a leather brown.

Finally, the storm broke up and the clouds drifted away, but there was still cattle up in them snow-covered mountains and Todd kept riding to get 'em down. He knowed that another storm would be the end of all the stock that was still there and if there was any left when it come, it sure wouldn't be his fault.

He kept a-riding out early in the morning and riding back on a mighty tired horse late at night. After taking care of his horse and disturbing the chink cook for something to eat, he'd hit for the bunk house and a few hours' rest. The fire was died down in there, the place was cold, and all the ranch hands was asleep. They'd still be asleep when the cowboy would get up, get a bite, and get out for another eighteen-hour ride.

After a few more days' hard riding, Todd finally brought down the last of the cattle; all of the herd was accounted for and down to where there was no more danger. That was no more than done when another storm, a good mate to the first one, came to pile on more snow. But there was no dread for Todd in that storm. His cattle was all down in the low country and amongst shelter and feed that'd carry 'em all thru any kind of winter.

When, after a few days, that second storm cleared, there was no sign of rocky ledges on the San Jacinto Mountains. They was all covered over and rounded out with many deep feet of hard-packed snow. Todd took a long breath at the sight and sort of smiled. He'd got his cattle down just in time.

But that cowboy wasn't thru with his work, and even tho his riding wouldn't keep him out for so long for some time to come, he had to be out plenty long enough, and with the short days of daylight that come at that time of the year, it was very seldom that he ever walked in the bunk house till it was night and dark had come.

It was as Todd was riding out for a usual day's circle, one morning, that the ranch foreman spotted him. He stood and watched the cowboy away for a spell and then he spoke to one of the ranch hands near him.

"It's the first time I've seen him in plain daylight for a long time," he remarked. Then after a while he went on: "It's dang queer about that feller. He'll ride horses I wouldn't touch with a forty-foot pole, in all kinds of weather, and for sometimes eighteen hours a day — but," he grinned, "*he won't work.*"